MISS FOR

A widowed earl, a governess who is far too clever for her own good, two motherless little girls, and one small dog who manages to bring them all together...

"Your First Kiss holds the answer to all that you desire." The fortune drew laughter from Matilda Fortune when Madame Zeta, a visiting gypsy uttered the ridiculous words.. At eight and twenty, Tilde's first kiss had long come and gone. As had the gentleman who bestowed it...

The Earl of Willoughby has given up on love. Since the death of his wife, he's lived in a fog. In route to London for the season, his mischievous daughters insist upon stopping at a small village. If only he hadn't allowed the mysterious gypsy to read his palm. Could his future be hidden in the past?

MISS FORTUNE'S FIRST KISS

ANNABELLE ANDERS

For Peaches.
And every pet who has ever brought joy to a child.

CHAPTER 1

MISFORTUNE

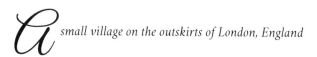

A small village on the outskirts of London, England

Your First Kiss holds the answer to all that you desire.

Tilde snorted with laughter as she walked out of the fortune teller's tent and into the sunshine on such a fine spring afternoon.

"Foolishness, Peaches, I tell you. Utter foolishness."

She chuckled again at her own words, aware that she was more likely to be judged to be foolish for talking to her dog. Nonetheless, loyal brown eyes stared up at her in complete agreement.

Peaches had been her small, short-legged, long-bodied companion for the past seven years. The sweet pup barely weighed half a stone and her coat varied between reddish browns and blacks. Tilde believed with all certainty that Peaches understood every word she said.

"*All* that I desire! Can you imagine, Peaches?" Tilde scoffed out loud.

But she could not prevent shelved memories from breaking through. She pondered the first time a man's lips had touched her own. A very long time ago. Eleven years this spring, to be exact. At one time, the old woman's words would have summoned tears.

Not that she'd been in love with him. Good Heavens, they'd only just met. It was just that she had been so sure he was … The One.

Perhaps, as a naïve and innocent girl, she'd concocted the magic. Imagined the certainty that she'd discovered the man of her dreams.

"Hello, dog." A shy voice drew Matilda's attention back to the present. "Will you bite me if I pet you?"

Matilda smiled down at the young girl. "Her name is Peaches and I think she'd quite enjoy being petted by such a well-mannered young lady." The child appeared to be five, maybe six, with silky black hair and pale skin. It seemed to have taken a great deal of courage for her to make her request. "But, come," Tilde suggested, mindful of the revelry going on all around them. "Let's step out of the path so no pedestrians trample us."

Both Peaches and the girl followed Tilde as she led them to a bench beside one of the tents. The little girl didn't seem to know what she ought to do next.

Since the earth was dry, Matilda lowered herself to the ground, wagering the three of them would all be more comfortable making introductions there. She gestured to the child, who immediately dropped down beside her.

"Peaches, this is… Pardon me, we failed to make our introductions to one another. My name is Miss Matilda Fortune." She dipped her head in lieu of dropping to a curtsey.

"I'm Althea." The child spoke the words timidly––to Peaches. Tilde's brows rose at the child's shyness and formal manner. By the quality of her dress and her perfectly braided and coiled hair, Matilda surmised Althea was no ordinary village urchin. Tilde glanced around and wondered where her nanny might be. She hoped she didn't draw anyone's ire by sitting with the girl in the dusty straw like this.

As soon as the thought came, however, she dismissed it. Children needed to be allowed to sit on the ground and play. They needed to be allowed to be *children*. Turning back to Peaches, she completed the proper introductions.

"You can touch her here." Tilde rubbed the back of Peaches' neck and lovingly worked her way down the dog's long body. "She especially likes it because she cannot scratch her own back."

Lady Althea raised her hands, which, in no time, were petting Peaches' short hair in long affectionate strokes. When Peaches deigned to lick the girl's chin, Althea giggled.

"Where is your nanny?" Again, Tilde twisted her head around to see if anyone appeared to be searching for someone. If the child was lost, then her charge would most certainly be looking for her.

They ought to be, anyhow!

"We don't have a nanny." Althea spoke without removing her gaze, or her hands, from Peaches.

"Did your mother bring you to the festival?" Tilde considered it highly unlikely that a peeress would attend such a common event.

But before Althea could answer, a virtual duplicate of her dropped onto the ground beside them. Lacking any of the shyness of her sister, the nearly indistinguishable looking girl began petting Peaches, who appeared to be in heaven.

"Althea! I've been looking all over for you! Is this your dog, Miss? Oh, he's a fine little fellow."

Little Althea mumbled inaudibly. Her sister--the girl had to be her sister, or even a twin—seemed to understand, nevertheless.

"You're tiny but you aren't a puppy, are you?" No bashfulness on this girl's part. "What's his name?"

Tilde drew herself up to her knees. If both girls were present, then *somebody* would soon find them. "She is a lady dog: Peaches. And yours? I take it you are Althea's sister?"

The second girl rose to her feet, all the while nodding. "I'm Eloise." And then she dropped into a perfect curtsey.

"I am Miss Matilda Fortune. It is, indeed, a pleasure to make your acquaintance."

Tilde didn't hold Eloise's attention for long.

Without warning, the child sprang into motion, shouting and waving her arms. "We're over here, Papa! Come see. Thea's found a dog!" With a sideways glance at Tilde, she added, "And a missus that owns it!"

Oh, dear. 'Papa' may not be at all too pleased with his daughters running off on their own. Tilde knew she most definitely would not.

And, she supposed, best not to be sitting cross-legged in the dirt if the gentleman was indeed, some sort of a lord. Unwinding her legs, Tilde pushed herself to her feet and then her full height. She couldn't quite make out his face but wished to reassure him of his daughters' well-being as quickly as possible. "They're safe and sound. And, I imagine, chockfull of apologies for worrying you."

She then clasped her hands in front of her, satisfied that these two little girls were no longer unsupervised. Although the village was a small one, country fairs like this often attracted more than a few undesirable characters.

None too pleased, the approaching man removed his hat, all the while scowling deeply at the four of them. These peers…

Without the brim of his hat pulled low, his long, aquiline nose, firm chin and unsmiling lips appeared quite distinguished. Tilde would have guessed him to be a gentleman even if she hadn't met the two little ladies first.

And then her breath caught.

Stormy gray eyes were lined with lashes, so black and thick he almost looked as though he'd rimmed them with kohl.

She'd seen those eyes before. And those lips.

Good Heavens! He was Jasper! It could not be. At this festival. Today. Of all days. She subdued her suddenly racing heart and ignored the heat creeping up her neck. His appearance here was merely an ironic coincidence. It was not some mystical twist of fate, foretold by a woman who claimed to have the second sight.

And that kiss had been so very long ago... *It's doubtful he remembers me.*

Judging by the look on his face, he wouldn't care if he had. In fact, no doubt all he felt was a mixture of relief and anger at his two lovely young daughters who'd managed to slip away from him.

A cheer arose as inhabitants of a nearby gaming tent chose that moment to celebrate some magnificent feat or other such nonsense. Peaches joined them merrily with a string of enthusiastic yaps. Further excited by the arrival of the girls' father, she began running in wild circles, twisting the leading string around Tilde's ankles. When the girls attempted to subdue her exuberant pet, more chaos ensued.

Likely he thinks we've all just stepped out of Bedlam.

And yet, Tilde refused to give into embarrassment. Of mind to bring some order to the situation, she moved to shush Peaches, but her entangled feet failed to cooperate. Despite waving her arms in an attempt to regain her balance, Tilde immediately realized this was not going to end well.

As she fell backward, the thick material of the tent wrapped itself around Tilde as the tent folded like an unstarched petticoat.

She winced as her bum hit the ground, but also at the shouted curses from the merchant who'd been inside.

Oh, dear. A most unfortunate turn of events.

It wasn't really necessary to greet him now, was it? The girl's father was with them now. They could go on their way with no fuss at all.

Perhaps Tilde could remain wrapped in the canvas for the duration of the afternoon. Or even crawl away undetected with Peaches in tow...

Because all she could think was that Jasper Talbot was the man the fortune teller spoke of. *All that you desire... First kiss...*

The fortune teller's prediction echoed in her head.

Eleven years before, he'd been the first man to ever kiss her.

* * *

A HALF HOUR after they arrived at the fair, Jasper Talbot, The Earl of Willoughby, was as far from amused as London is from Calcutta. First his daughters had demanded they delay their journey to stop for the festival. Then they had immediately bolted out of sight, causing him no small amount of worry.

They could have been driving into Mayfair about now if he wasn't so easily manipulated by his little urchins.

Cheers sounded from some sort of strength competition up ahead. Had his daughters not gone missing, he wouldn't have minded a look at the show. A decade ago, his brash self might even have accepted the challenge. But for now, he needed to assure himself of their safety. God help him if anything ever happened to those two imps.

They would be fine, of course. They likely got distracted by a tent filled with baubles.

A waft of manure drifted through the alley of vendors. Booths featuring animals would have captured his daughter's attention as well. Willoughby wrinkled his nose in disgust when he passed a pen holding a giant hog. It wasn't that he took issue with farm animal smells, but he did when they were directly adjacent to a tent selling meat pies.

Where are they?

Lengthening his stride, he flicked his gaze left and right. He'd ordered them to remain close. It would serve them right if he took the strap to their tiny behinds.

Except he'd never do such a thing.

A flapping pastel pink ribbon drew his attention, granting him no small amount of relief. On the dirt, in their pretty dresses with what looked to be––what he *hoped* to be anyhow––a *dog*, his daughters sat merrily playing. They were annoyingly oblivious to the panic they'd caused him.

He did not shout their names but instead marched determinedly in that direction. The two dark heads were bent over, intently focused upon the mongrel.

And then one of the girls glanced up. Eloise, of course. Althea spent an inordinate amount of time living within her own mind, a dreamland of sorts, uninterested in the world around her.

"We're over here, Papa! Come see, Thea's found a dog!" She twisted her lips into a grimace before adding, "And a missus that owns it!"

The dog's owner––a spinster if he were to guess from her unfashionable attire––pushed herself off the ground as he approached. He was, indeed, grateful that she'd kept the girls in one place long enough that he could find them. He only hoped she didn't take it upon herself to admonish his parenting.

Or lack, thereof.

The governess he intended to hire wasn't to start until next week, and that wouldn't be a moment too soon.

"They're safe and sound and, I imagine, filled with apologies for worrying you."

He half noted the spinster's voluptuous curves with disdain. The material of her dress was faded and worn. Atop her head she'd perched a straw hat ornamented with flowers and what appeared to be… bumble bees.

But then the woman's face caught and held his attention. Something familiar about her. Upturned nose, full rosy lips and eyes that were… brown, perhaps? As they widened in shock, they appeared more of an olive tone.

He'd definitely met this woman before...

More cheers from the revelers broke into his train of thought. She went to quiet her dog as he approached. "Have a care, madam!" He shouted too late.

Before he could do anything to prevent certain calamity, the blasted woman had lost her balance and fallen backwards into the precarious structure. His girls looked on in astonishment while the entire apparatus collapsed to the ground.

And then.

Silence.

"Misfortune?" Eloise took a timid step toward the pile of canvas that had swallowed the woman whole. Unfortunate indeed.

"You must help her, Papa!" Eloise implored him as though the woman had fallen into some great abyss. "You have to save her! What if she cannot breathe?"

"I'm certain she can breathe."

But Althea begged him with soulful eyes.

Dropping to his haunches, he began unwrapping the blasted woman, fold by fold. With one final tug he revealed her inert form.

She lay in repose, as though the fall had indeed killed her. One glance at her bosom, rising and falling, assured him that it had not.

Rather generous bosom.

His gaze travelled upward, and a recollection tantalized his mind as he noticed golden red strands shining in her chestnut hair. Long, thick lashes fanned out against her flushed complexion. And such full lips, he'd not known since…

"Miss Fortune?" Eloise dropped to her knees beside him.

"Misfortune?" He questioned. "Calm down, Eloise, I believe she yet lives."

"No, Papa. That's her name. *Miss* Fortune. *Matilde Fortune.*"

He'd heard that name before. "Miss Fortune." It felt familiar on his lips as he touched the woman's shoulder. "Are you injured?"

She opened her eyes, and then raised a hand to shade the sun from them.

"Only my pride," she admitted with a rueful smile. Miss Fortune wasn't a beauty by societal standards, but her smile generated a surprising energy inside of him. Taking her hand, he tugged her so that she could sit up. "Oh, but I've made a mess!"

She had indeed, and yet, he sensed laughter could overflow from her any moment.

"You're sorry, aren't you, Peaches?" Althea stepped forward, cradling the pup in her arms. As she cuddled the tiny head beneath her chin, she glanced sideways at her father defiantly.

Miss Fortune made a clucking sound with her tongue. "Naughty, naughty Peaches! She forgot her manners, didn't she? I'm so glad you could comfort her. She isn't used to being around quite so many people at once. She certainly likes you, Althea."

His daughter nodded solemnly and then a hint of a smile danced on her lips.

This––Miss Fortune woman––had cast some sort of spell on all of them.

Had this been Eloise, he wouldn't have been surprised at the behavior at all. But to see his painfully shy sweetheart having a perfectly normal conversation with a stranger…

He swallowed hard and turned back to the woman still sitting in the crumpled canvas of the collapsed tent. Only then did he realize he still clasped her hand in his. He dropped it and then immediately experienced an odd sensation of loss.

At sixes and sevens, Jasper held her gaze and was once again caught in the feeling that he'd known her.

And before he could offer further assistance, she'd brushed at her skirt, swung her feet around and pushed herself off the ground.

Rising himself, he glanced at his daughters and then back at Miss Fortune.

One would think a person, having displayed such undignified behavior, would have the decency to look ashamed.

Not this one.

Putting the entire incident behind her, she immediately began sounding more like the busybody he'd initially taken her for.

"You girls ought not to have left your father's side. I would be devastated if Peaches ran away from me, absolutely heartbroken. I imagine your father felt even worse." Both girls nodded solemnly.

She glanced back at him, but only for a moment, taking the opportunity to lift Peaches from Althea's arms and inspecting the knot on the leading string. "Now that these two are safe and sound, Peaches and I had best be on our way. You two girls be good."

And then one more glance in his direction. "Your daughters really ought to have a nanny, or a governess. They're naturally curious and a good teacher will keep their minds occupied and less likely to find trouble."

Jasper straightened his spine, irritated at being advised by a perfect stranger. Not that it was any of her business, but a new governess awaited the girls in London. What manner of idiot did she take him for?

He merely tipped his hat. "Nonetheless, madam, I thank you for your assistance."

She held his gaze, only for a moment. Her lips parted as though she had something more to say, but then closed tight again.

She nodded. "You are quite welcome."

And then, after allowing the girls to say goodbye to her

absurd excuse for a dog, head held high with that ridiculous hat, she marched away from them all.

Jasper's gaze followed the motion of her hips until they disappeared into the throngs of carnival merrymakers. Busybody or not, there was something about that woman…

CHAPTER 2

REMINISCING

*H*olding both his girls' hands, Jasper shook off the sense of melancholy threatening to settle over him.

"We'd best get back to the carriage now." He'd had enough of this particular village and its carnival.

"But Papa, we only just arrived!" Eloise complained.

"You girls took ten years off my life for disappearing like that." Jasper experienced very little trouble in most aspects of his life; when not managing his girls, that was. With this in mind, he scowled down at his daughters.

And it made no difference to the little imps whatsoever.

"It wasn't my fault. I simply had to go after Althea. Would you have preferred I didn't bother following her? We might have lost her forever, Papa! But if that's what you'd prefer…" She shrugged innocently and batted her lashes at him.

"You should simply have told me."

"But you were speaking with Coachman John."

It seemed he could never win any arguments with Eloise. Closing his eyes briefly, he summoned an added measure of patience. Jasper loved his daughters more than anything in the world, if something were to happen to one of them... He swallowed hard and secured his hold on each tiny hand.

Intent on getting them back to the safety of the carriage, he took a deep breath and then careful not to loosen his grip, began ushering his two escape artists between the cacophony of exhibits and tents.

"A penny to hear your fortune!" A woman draped in colorful scarves beckoned to passersby. He lengthened his stride, practically dragging the girls beside him. The woman lifted her hand and pointed. "You, sir. Wouldn't you like to know what lies ahead for you and your daughters?"

Utter nonsense.

And yet, a chill ran down his spine.

And of course, Eloise began jumping up and down. "Do it, Papa! And then we can leave! Look at her dress. Isn't it pretty? You need to find out what our futures are, Papa. And then can we get a puppy? One like Peaches?"

Althea remained silent but tugged at his other arm. He paused in his steps and exhaled a long slow breath.

Daughters.

The fortune was only a penny. If he appeased them in this one thing, they could then be on their way.

"We'll do the fortune, but not the puppy."

Eloise squealed and Althea frowned.

The fortuneteller waved them over to a smaller tent. It had a banner with the words 'Madame Zeta' hung across the opening. As they followed her, the scent of burning incense met his nostrils and his eyes required adjusting to the dim light inside.

He ought not to have given into Eloise.

Again.

"Sit here." She pointed out a chair for him and another for the girls to share. Both of his daughters appeared quite fascinated by the woman, with all her rings, and earbobs and necklaces. Her eyes, a greyish blue color, contrasted vividly with the woman's dark skin and black hair peeking out from beneath her scarves. Candlelight flickered eerily, creating long shadows on the tent walls as a gust of wind shook the transient structure.

"What is your necklace?" Eloise pointed toward a charm hanging on the longest chain around Madame Zeta's neck.

The woman smiled at his daughter, however, and held the charm out to Eloise and Althea for closer inspection. "It was given to me by my Mama, when I was your very same age." And then she pointed out the circling lines and swirls. "It is the path of life and it is a secret charm for ladies."

More nonsense.

When she spoke the words, she stared across the room at him. "Fate reveals choices to all of us. Our fortune awaits us in the path we take." Her voice had lowered, with a hint of some accent he didn't recognize.

"It's pretty." Eloise spoke the words in awe. Althea watched the woman with wide eyes. Likely now, the fortune teller would offer to sell it to him. She probably had dozens of others hidden away.

Enough was enough. He began to rise.

"You, sir." She paused for dramatic affect. "Give. Hand. Now."

Shaken by her bold declaration, he nonetheless held out his hand for her to take. She trailed her gnarled finger along his palm and then closed her eyes and inhaled deeply.

"The secret to finding your future lies in the fortune you lost in your past."

She dropped his hand as though it had suddenly turned to fire.

He'd managed to do nothing but amass tremendous wealth over the entire course of his life. Unwilling to waste any more time, he stood and reached into his pocket to withdraw a few coins. "We thank you for your time, Madame Zeta."

And for once, the girls did not resist him as they exited back into the sunlight and walked the distance to the travelling carriage awaiting them.

"What's fate, Papa?" And, "Did you really lose something in your past?"

"Fate is for people who fail to order their own lives to their betterment." He answered Eloise's question. "And no, I've not misplaced a fortune. Unless you count my daughters, who are forever getting themselves lost by running off without permission."

He lifted her into the carriage and turned back toward his other daughter.

"Papa, when can we get a dog?" Eloise seemed to have forgotten that he'd already given her an answer. She'd become quite good at that, forgetting his answer when it wasn't the one she wanted to hear.

"Let's get you a governess, first, shall we?"

* * *

TILDE STARED out the carriage window at the passing scenery.

For all of thirty seconds, she'd wondered if there had been some truth in the fortuneteller's words.

But of course, there had not been. He was obviously married.

She had nearly said something––in that last moment––to remind him, but then caught herself. It would have been embarrassing if he had failed to remember her, even after prompting. Then again, there might have been even more embarrassment if he *had*, in fact, remembered. She hadn't exactly behaved demurely that night. Heat seeped up her neck at the memory.

He'd demonstrated no signs of recognizing her. Perhaps she been mistaken? After all, eleven years was a very long time. Was it possible she'd incorrectly assumed a similar looking man was him? She'd been prompted by the fortuneteller to recall her first kiss and he had most certainly been foremost in her mind. Had she simply erroneously assumed the first man to come along was Jasper Talbot? One evening. She'd known him for but a matter of a few hours. It was possible, she supposed.

But not probable.

More likely, Althea and Eloise's father was one of Jasper's relatives; a cousin, or brother perhaps. That would explain the strong resemblance.

But no.

Deep in her heart, she knew she had not been mistaken.

His voice. His eyes. The way her heart skipped a beat at his touch.

He could only be Jasper. He'd simply failed to remember her.

A wheel hit a rut and she clutched the leather strap on the wall tightly.

Tilde sighed. Life was like that, filled with ruts and bumps one simply needed to endure. The young ladies she had been charged with for the past several years had grown. They no longer required a governess. In a gesture of appreciation, Lord and Lady Brightly, her former employers, had been quite kind in providing transportation so that she hadn't been obliged to take the mail coach.

She wondered if she'd ever see the family again. She might, she supposed. Anything was possible…

Over the past decade, she'd occasionally allowed her mind to conjure the memory of that night. She'd always speculated where Jasper's life had taken him, whether or not he'd found happiness.

Or if he was even alive. For all she knew, he could have perished in the war, or taken ill. It wasn't as though she'd ever heard from him again…

She chuckled to herself.

She had not been mistaken.

He was most definitely alive. And more handsome now than before. The line of his jaw had grown firmer. His arrogance had matured as well.

She released a melancholy sigh.

He'd been brashly confident eleven years ago, in a young, almost impatient, sense. Now his arrogance had hardened into that of a man who knew himself.

And yet.

She'd thought she'd recognized sadness in his eyes. Eyes mirrored in his daughters' faces.

Twin girls. One confident and talkative, and the other quiet and shy. The three of them together seemed… lost.

As though sensing her thoughts, Peaches edged up from her lap in order to nuzzle Tilde beneath her chin. She dropped a kiss upon the soft short hairs of her faithful companion's head.

The entire scenario of events had been quite unfortunate.

She grimaced at the irony. An unfortunate fortune for Matilda Fortune.

Stop feeling sorry for yourself, Matilda.

She straightened her spine. Self-pity never proved to be anything but an exercise in futility and she refused to take part in it.

She'd spent the past decade shaping the lives of three lovely girls. She had the honor of teaching them, and then watching them blossom into beautiful young women. The time had come, however, to move onto something different, to embrace a new future. Already, the employment agency said they had a most enviable position available. They'd said her references were impeccable. The Baroness had sent them a glowing recommendation.

And next week she would interview her new potential 'family.' If they failed to meet her standards, she'd simply inform the agency and await another opportunity. She knew of her worth, what with many of her ladyship's acquaintances having attempted to lure her away. Tilde would not enter a situation that wasn't a good fit.

Before taking up her new position, however, she would spend

some treasured time with her aunt and the eldest of her three younger sisters, Betsy.

Her other two sisters, Chloe and Charlotte, were currently at Miss Primm's Ladies' Seminary. When Chloe graduated, she'd been offered a position straightaway as a teacher. Charlotte, not quite seventeen, remained a student.

Betsy was only two years younger than Matilda. She acted as companion for Aunt Nellie, who'd taken all of them in upon their parents' death.

Tilde looked forward to simply being at home, with no responsibilities, for all of five days. She could visit a few museums, see the menagerie, and sit in Hyde Park late in the day and quietly observe the members of the ton fawn over themselves. People watching was one of her favorite pastimes while in London.

And then a thought struck her.

It was quite possible that Jasper Talbot would be one of them.

Before she'd realized that it was he, she'd guessed Althea and Eloise's parents to be peers of some sort. And this time of year, all the peers who wished to be seen were returning to London for the Season.

It was possible he'd inherited a title of some sort and if that was the case, he'd move socially amongst the crème de la crème. He certainly exhibited the arrogance of one of London's elite.

Eleven years ago, he'd simply been Mr. Talbot to her.

Jasper.

She and her parents had been invited to join one of her father's friends for an evening at Vauxhall. They'd crossed to the Gardens via boat, and Tilde had been in more than a little awe over the flowers, the music, and the ubiquitous colorful lanterns. And of course, the people, from all walks of life.

Her father hadn't been wealthy, but he'd been a landowner and wasn't a pauper either. Unfortunately, his wife had only presented him with daughters. His four little misfortunes, he used to joke. When he and her mother had been killed, their small estate had passed to Father's younger brother, Mr. Colin Fortune. A most disagreeable man.

A great deal had changed after her parents' death.

Feeling the loss of long ago, Tilde dipped her chin and kissed the top of Peaches' head.

That spring had most certainly presented Tilde and her sisters with their fair share of bumps and ruts, or more aptly, mountains and canyons.

The high point for Tilde, indeed, had been meeting Jasper and experiencing her first kiss.

Sitting in their host's supper box in the midst of all that was pleasurable, she and Jasper had noticed one another before even being introduced. She'd only pretended to eat the strawberries and thinly shaved meats after catching him staring at her more than once. Never had she met a more dashing gentleman––in all of her seventeen years.

She'd been unable to keep from staring back.

And eventually, he acknowledged interest. A slight upturn of his lips. A smile.

She'd blushed and dipped her head, but then glanced up again, and returned an oh, so very demure smile in his direction.

He'd been a handsome young man but there had been something else... Something almost magical. In the midst of the fairyland setting, she'd felt as though an imaginary spider was weaving a silken web around the two of them, leaving neither the choice but to eventually come together.

Chaperones had been lax as the evening wore on. When he'd asked her if she'd like to go walking, she'd eagerly accepted. She'd not taken his arm, she remembered, but walked alongside of him with her hands behind her back.

Neither had seemed to notice the various vendors along the way, or the music, or the dancers. They took turns asking one

ANNABELLE ANDERS

another questions, but the answers didn't really matter. All that had mattered was the thick attraction building between them.

It had felt like a physical thing.

Tilde hadn't thought of it for a long time, but even now, years later, she remembered the weight of it.

They'd been destined to come together.

To kiss.

And at the time, she'd thought… so much more.

* * *

Jasper stared out the window as his elegant coach rambled into the heart of London. The girls were both sleeping. Eloise was on the rear facing bench, and Althea was beside him, resting her head on his lap. He abstractly threaded his fingers through the downy softness of her hair, black, identical to his.

How had he not recognized her right away? Tilde. Matilda. She'd been introduced to him as Miss Fortune. At Vauxhall, just a few weeks before he'd met Estelle.

Had she remembered? Or had he merely seemed familiar to her, as well.

Eleven years.

A lifetime.

He recalled that he'd considered her beautiful. She hadn't been, even then, but she'd affected him as no other woman up until that point in his life.

She had been pretty, but it had been her eyes that captured him. Smiling, mischievous and daring eyes––so out of place on the face of a young debutante. She'd not been forward, nor acted inappropriately in any way. She'd merely had this *look* to her… As though daring life to upset her joy.

They'd walked together through the lantern-lit paths.

He smiled sadly to himself. Throughout the course of one's youth, a person happens upon magical moments without realizing how uniquely special they were. That was how he remembered that night.

As he'd grown older, he'd dismissed it as something nonsensical. There had been champagne and wine, yes, but he'd had his wits about him.

She'd taken his arm when he turned them onto a darker, less travelled path. And he'd flirted with her and teased her about her name.

Miss Fortune.

"Matilda," she'd said, "but my friends call me Tilde."

"Tilde then. And you must call me Jasper."

He shook his head at his impetuous attitudes back then. His own wife had hardly ever referred to him by anything other than Willoughby. And his closest of friends, called him Will. He'd come into the title while still in school. It had been freeing to cast the mantle away for a night. To have a pretty girl like *him*, not the earldom.

He'd thrilled when she'd tested his name on her lips.

Jasper.

Had she recognized him today? Surely his appearance wasn't so very greatly altered.

Eleven years. Ah, but yes, a lifetime ago.

Tilde had crossed his path like a mirage. He'd kissed her. Oh, yes. He'd led her into the dark forest and then off the path altogether. She'd leaned against the smooth bark of a tree. She'd not been acting coquettish, no, they'd been enjoying one another's company.

Immensely.

And then he'd covered the empty space between the two of them and placed his hands on the tree, above her head. Both of them had stared into one another's eyes, not touching, but... feeling. Feeling the visceral energy sparking between their bodies.

His, lean and hard. Hers, yielding and soft.

He'd inhaled her perfume, thinking to memorize it. Shaking

his head, he smiled ruefully to himself. Although he remembered how the fragrance had made him feel, he could not remember the fragrance itself.

"I can't tell if your eyes are brown or green."

She'd gazed up at him and licked her lips. "Hazel."

"Lovely," he'd whispered. He remembered how hoarse his voice had sounded.

He'd been utterly besotted with her.

Jasper shifted on his seat, careful not to wake Althea. When he glanced out the window once again, he was surprised to realize they'd already driven as far as Mayfair. They'd arrive in mere minutes now.

"Wake up, lovelies." He reached across and shook Eloise gently. "We're home."

CHAPTER 3

MOTHERS AND SISTERS

London, England Spring of 1821

"Willoughby, darling! I expected you to arrive yesterday." The greeting came as no surprise. Placing one hand
on each of his daughters' shoulders, Jasper gave an encouraging
squeeze and then ushered them into the darkened drawing room.

"Hello, Mother. Make your curtseys to your grandmother,
girls."

Eloise stepped forward first and dropped into an exaggerated
curtsey that she'd obviously practiced.

Althea backed up and seemed to have frozen in place.

"Step forward, girl." Hester Talbot, the most honorable Lady
Willoughby, bit out the command. "I still don't understand why
you bring them to London with you. They'll likely only prove to
be a nuisance."

Jasper bent forward. "You can do it." He whispered into
Althea's ear before nudging her forward gently. Her curtsey
lacked all of the flair of Eloise's but managed to pass muster none
the less.

"We're to meet with a possible governor for them, as I
informed you in my letter." He hated that he had to explain this

in front of his daughters. He didn't want them to think he would have preferred leaving them in the country to be cared for by servants. He caught Althea's watchful eyes and winked. "And I promised to take them to Gunter's."

"Nonetheless," his mother reached for the bell pull, "I've had the nursery aired out and made other arrangements until this governess of yours sees fit to begin her duties. Whatever were you thinking, Willoughby? You'll be far too busy meeting prospective brides to waste time playing nursemaid."

"Did I tell you that Marvelle's daughter is having her come out tomorrow night? Promises to be a crush. Lady Elaine is such a lovely young woman. The duchess has invited everyone who is anyone. I assured her you would want to reserve Lady Elaine's first dance. An honor to be certain. Shall I send your request around in the morning?"

Jasper blinked as he attempted to follow his mother's train of thought. A matronly looking woman appeared in the open doorway.

"Take the children up to the nursery now, Miss Bates. That will be all."

His daughters glanced over at him quickly. He really was going to have to curtail his mother's... suggestions. Lifting a halting hand toward the maid, he crouched down to his daughters' level. "There's piles of toys upstairs, if I remember correctly. I'll be up to help you get settled in after I've finished talking with your grandmother." He knew his mother all too well. If she were to have her way, he wouldn't see his daughters again until they were at least six and ten. "And then we'll all take supper together."

"Willoughby–" his mother began.

"Run along and allow Miss Bates to assist you out of your travelling dresses into something fresh to dine in."

Althea bit her lip and nodded, but Eloise continued watching him skeptically. That look sent a sharp ache into his heart.

The servant efficiently took both girls hands and led them out of the room. When the door closed behind her, Jasper ran one hand through his hair and sighed. "It's been little more than a year, Mother."

"They're not infants."

The darkness his mother preferred frustrated him. Unwilling to tolerate it a moment longer, he crossed the room and swept open a thick and heavy curtain. His mother turned her head away. "You know how I hate the glare."

She rarely went out in the daylight and he was beginning to understand why. Not that her appearance changed the way he felt about her. She was his mother, after all.

But the powder and paints failed to conceal the creases that had developed on her face. She'd always been a harsh woman, and the lines about her mouth provided further evidence of it. Almost all of her hair had turned white. Nearly seventy now, she'd given birth to him late in life. She'd refused to give up in her efforts to provide his father with an heir despite several miscarriages earlier on.

And yet she did not appear frail. His mother would never appear frail.

"How are you, Mother?" Did he wish to know? Would she tell him anything besides the obvious?

"Delighted, now that you've arrived. I've done nothing but worry that you'd remain hidden away in the country. You're a young man, my darling, but you are also Willoughby. You cannot forget your responsibility to provide for the future of the Earldom. Estelle was a beautiful girl, but she was never the same after the twins were born. Likely, her illness was something of a blessing in disguise."

"You'll never utter such sentiments in my daughters' presence, and you'll do well to not do so again in mine as well. *She was my wife.*" He bit his tongue to prevent himself from saying more.

"And I am your mother." She made a tutting sound. "Now

25

come sit down. I've several invitations to go over with you. And also, my list."

"Of festivities you wish to attend?"

She laughed. "Of course not, Willoughby. I've already decided which of those you'll make an appearance. No, my list of prospective wives for you. I've vetoed the unhealthy-looking ones, the ugly ones, the ones with controlling mothers, and those who might be trouble. You've absented yourself from London for far too long. You'll do well to take my advice."

Jasper ran his hand through his hair once again before taking the seat beside her. "I'll hire the girls a governess first." He promised. "And then I'll see about finding them a mother."

His mother cackled. "It's not a mother for the twins that I'm concerned about, Willoughby. What matters most is that you find a mother for your sons."

* * *

TILDE'S AUNT NETTIE, already dressed and coiffured as though she were attending a garden party, set her cup of tea beside her still full breakfast plate. "I forgot all about this one, but Lady Abbot says it's going to be quite the crush. Apparently, the Duchess of Marvelle has sent out hundreds of invitations. I realize it's late notice, but I suppose we ought to attend." Matilda had been in London for four days now. After visiting the menagerie, the Royal Academy of Arts Museum, doing some shopping on Bond Street and buying ices at Gunter's two days in a row, she was feeling refreshed and enthusiastic to settle into a new post.

She'd squashed all thoughts of Jasper into the deep recesses of her brain, refusing to imagine who he'd married, where he lived, whether or not he was in London, or if she'd see him again…

She'd not allowed herself to contemplate such ridiculous

questions on her part. She couldn't afford the melancholy, or the regret.

Or the hurt.

"Shall we attend then, Tilde?"

"Who? Attend what?" Tilde hadn't been paying attention.

"I imagine it will be quite grand." Betsy was only two years younger than Tilde but often had the outlook of a person twice her age. She'd not done well at school and when her fiancé died tragically seven years before, she'd fallen into a great despair and declared she would never marry.

Aunt Nellie hadn't questioned Betsy's decision, or those of any of the Fortune sisters for that matter, but Tilde secretly believed her aunt had not given up hope of finding husbands for them all.

"I'd think you'd enjoy partaking of a little entertainment before stepping into your new post." Mrs. Nellie Maisley, although neither wealthy, nor of noble birth, was something of a fixture amongst the ton. She'd married the second son of a viscount and then outlived all but the most recent heir, a distant nephew twice––or perhaps it was thrice? ––removed. Although she no longer had direct access to the family coffers, aside from a measly widow's portion, she retained a fabulous array of outmoded dresses and a slowly dwindling collection of jewelry. None had ever dared to question Aunt Nellie as mistress of her London townhouse.

She received invitations quite often and, in the past, had taken her nieces along. Lacking any sort of dowry or great claims to beauty, Betsy, Chloe and Tilde often found themselves consigned almost immediately to the wallflower seating where their remade dresses weren't as noticeable.

All in all, aside from Betsy's short engagement to Mr. Joseph Fitzwilliam, the orphaned sisters hadn't fared well amongst Society.

Which was partially why Tilde had emphasized that all of her sisters make the most of their educations.

Tilde had completed her schooling just before her parents' death and entered into service after two failed Seasons. Once employed, Tilde had paid for most of Chloe's schooling and then Charlotte's, the youngest, who at the age of ten and six was nearing the end of her education at Miss Primm's. She'd complained on more than one occasion, however, at having Chloe as one of her teachers.

Miss Primm's was a special school. They'd all been quite fortunate to have attended. If only Betsy hadn't hated it so…

"What do you think Matilda?"

Tilde jerked her chin up. "Of what?"

"Shall we attend the Duchess of Marvelle's Ball?"

Tilde had not planned on attending a ton event ever again. She was in service now. It would be embarrassing to come face to face with one of her prior employer's family members, or even one of their acquaintances who'd observed her. Just as she thought to decline, however, she caught a wistful expression on her sister's face, as though she'd been waiting for just such an opportunity.

Betsy could attend alone with Aunt Nellie, but likely, that would not be the same as going with her older sister.

"Tonight?"

Betsy smiled and nodded.

"But… I've nothing to wear."

As though taking this as only a minor impediment, Betsy clasped her hands together. "Oh, but I've the perfect gown for you. It will be like old times––"

Tilde laughed. "You and I, sitting together with all the other chaperones and wallflowers."

Betsy grimaced. "We'll have fun." She then dropped her napkin onto the table and pushed back her chair. "If you've no objections then, we've no time to waste! I'll pull out the gown and you can try it on right away. That will give me plenty of time to make any necessary alterations."

"But I––"

"And I've a new style to try with your hair. And you can do mine!"

Tilde gave in with a sigh and stabbed her eggs with more force than necessary. It would likely be her last opportunity to dress up and mingle in elegant society in her own right, for a very long time. More likely, forever.

And then Betsy—sober-minded, quiet Betsy—squealed. "Come up as soon as you've finished!"

In the quiet that remained after Betsy's departure, Tilde glanced at her aunt with questioning eyes. Aunt Nellie smiled secretly. "Your sister has been working very hard."

CHAPTER 4

WHAT A BALL!

*J*asper eased into the hot water and leaned his head back while his valet moved efficiently around the room. On days such as this one, he felt more than at least twice his age. What aged him wasn't the physical challenges of life, however, but the mental ones. Most specifically, being the father to two six-year-old little girls. One who seemed afraid of the world, and the other afraid for the sibling she's determined to protect at all costs.

Since arriving in London, Jasper had met with three different governesses. The first lady had been far too young and naïve for him to trust. The second had been so very old that he doubted she would have been able to keep up with the girls. The third he'd known immediately would be far too strict.

His mother had quite approved of her.

The agency promised they had the perfect lady and would be sending her over the next day. In the meantime, his mother had made promises on his behalf that he'd not had the heart to break.

The Duke of Marvelle's daughter, indeed, was quite lovely. He'd squired her while shopping, to a musicale and to two garden parties already.

Of course, his mother had promised that he'd lead the young woman in her first dance at the ball that evening. He hated to imagine what his mother would have done if he'd delayed his arrival by even a week or cancelled it outright. He needed to be careful not to give rise to any expectations he wasn't prepared to fulfill. Although, likely, his mother already had done so on his part.

He closed his eyes while Cummings, his valet of nearly fifteen years, brushed warm shaving cream onto his jaw and neck.

His wife had barely been in the ground a year. How could his mother expect he'd be ready to marry again already?

"Relax, my lord." Cummings withdrew the razor from Willoughby's face. "I don't want to cut you where you're clenching your jaw."

Last time the valet had drawn blood, Cummings had been mortified. He had nearly resigned in humiliation. If Jasper remembered correctly, his mother had been the cause of his irritation on that occasion as well. He exhaled determinedly. "Carry on."

He was not prepared to marry again so soon. Marriage had involved a great deal of... work, compromise, disappointment and then grief.

The first few years he'd done his best to keep Estelle happy. She'd been a good woman. Matters likely wouldn't have deteriorated so much had they not failed to conceive in the first year of their marriage, nor their second. They'd all but given up until she'd announced to him that she was expecting. It had been one of the last times they'd seemed happy together. They'd been celebrating their fourth wedding anniversary.

He'd been ecstatic. They'd all had such high expectations for the blessed event. But early on in her pregnancy, Estelle had taken to her bed. She'd often appeared pale and tired and had struggled to keep her meals down. She'd reassured him that she was fine. Nonetheless, when the girls were finally born, they all breathed a sigh of relief.

It was short-lived.

The girls were barely a month old when Estelle had begun making apologies for not bearing him an heir. She'd been raised a duke's daughter and considered it her duty. Her disappointment in herself had opened a fault in their marriage. No matter what he'd done or said, she could not allow herself to be happy. Nor could she be happy with their girls.

Good God, her final words on this earth had been an apology to him.

Finished with the shave, Cummings covered Jasper's face with a towel and removed the excess shaving soap. "I've laid out both your amber and your evergreen waistcoat. Have you a preference, my lord?"

Jasper wasn't eager for any of this. Instead of answering, he held his breath while the valet poured warm water over him, and then shook his head vigorously, sending water flying.

"No colors, Cummings. Black."

The same as his mood.

* * *

APPARENTLY, in her spare time, Betsy sewed.

Not only sewed but created magnificent designs and then managed to make them come to life from Aunt Nellie's collection. Her sister had, indeed, been very busy since Tilde had last been home.

And she'd created one specifically for her.

It was made of a luxurious silk patterned with tiny blue flowers. The bodice revealed slightly more bosom than Tilde preferred, but she could hardly complain. And the skirt didn't merely fall to the floor, it streamed down the length of her body, catching the curve of her hip as she walked without being flagrantly revealing.

The gown did not require an abundance of ribbons or lace. In fact, there wasn't any. All of the elegance and beauty came from the cut and the style.

It truly was a work of art.

As soon as Tilde glanced in the mirror, she realized why her sister had been so excited to attend the Duchess of Marvelle's ball.

Who wouldn't wish to show off something so beautiful? Betsy could not wear it herself. She had sewn it to Tilde's measurements, which were somewhat bigger than her younger sister's.

"You knew of the invitation weeks before. You must have." Tilde stared over her shoulder to try to catch a glimpse of the back of the gown. "I knew that you could sew, but I never would have expected…" Tilde twirled around twice, "this."

Betsy smiled smugly. "I don't want to merely sew in another lady's shop," she spoke in earnest. "I want to own my own. I've made tons of drawings, designs. Aunt Nellie says if she had any extra money, she'd help but… and I know how you feel about that. But I thought if one of the ladies at the ball saw the gown, and perhaps decided she'd like one for herself. Well, I thought I could make dresses from here and save up."

Tilde couldn't help but smile. She'd known Betsy couldn't be happy forever acting as her aunt's companion. Perhaps she hadn't done well at school, but she certainly hadn't ever been feeble minded.

Betsy fashioned Tilde's hair into an elaborate updo with braids and curls. Then Betsy dressed herself in a second gown, a similar creation in amethyst taffeta.

Her sister impressed her to no end.

Aunt Nellie nodded in approval as they climbed into her ancient carriage. Marvelle House was a Palladian mansion across from Hyde Park. It appeared like a Greek temple set amongst the rows of townhouses. It stood three stories high and ornately carved columns flanked the large front entryway. Numerous coaches, some shiny and new, and others more weathered, lined up to set down their passengers onto the carpet rolled out to the pavement.

Tilde's breath caught when she glimpsed the back of a gentleman wearing a similar hat to Jasper's. When the figure turned to reveal himself a considerably younger man, relief swept through her.

As well as disappointment.

She'd known it would be possible he'd be in attendance, but assured herself that, if he was indeed, a peer, he'd mingle with other titled ladies and gentlemen and would have no cause to peruse the faces of ladies seated against the wall. After alighting from their own carriage, Aunt Nellie, Betsy and Tilde waited in the long receiving line before making their curtsies to their host and hostess, and the young woman being presented to society.

Barely seventeen, Lady Elaine, the daughter of the Duke and Duchess of Marvelle, caused all other ladies to fade into near obscurity. And by the look in her eyes, she knew it.

The girl wore an impressive tiara and a gown which might as well have been threaded together with golden strands. Her debut ball was grand, but her beauty was Hellenic. And she would surely smile to see a thousand ships sail out to war over her favors.

Tilde and Betsy had glanced sideways at one another, in a knowing sisterly way, and then dropped into curtseys before the girl. After the very brief introduction, they, along with Aunt Nellie, moved along to be announced and then await the beginning of the music in an ornately decorated ballroom. Hundreds of candles flickered above in enormous chandeliers illuminating the ubiquitous gold ribbons and white flowers strategically placed within.

Tilde had difficulty imagining going to such great expense for a seventeen-year-old girl. It was the way of this world though. Likely, the young woman would go on to become a duchess herself. At the very least, a countess.

It felt like almost no time had passed since the brief period all those years ago, when they'd mingled amongst the ton. Tilde and Betsy escorted their aunt to where a cluster of her cronies were seated, and then crept around the edge of the room to the long line of chairs backed up against the wall.

"But we must remain standing," Betsy insisted, "in order to show my gowns to their best advantage."

Tilde laughed. She appreciated that they were to have a purpose for attending. They were not debutantes, nor married ladies. They were the least envied of all in attendance: spinsters.

Betsy's gaze roved around the room and then grimaced. And then, as though she'd read Tilde's mind, "We're spinsters now, Tilde."

"Indeed." But Tilde smiled. "Why couldn't the word for an unmarried woman be something a little less harsh sounding? Spin–ster. Like a Bannister. Or a Spectator."

"Tincture." Betsy added. And it soon became a game.

"Ladies who elect not to marry ought to be called something else… Like…"

"Satin. Or twilight. Or Destiny." Betsy offered, a grin dancing on her mouth.

"Twilight implies aged. What about Amnesty?"

"Amnesty?"

"The implication that all is forgiven, and we chose to go forward as single ladies."

Betsy nodded. "I like it. From this day forward we shall refer to ourselves as amnesties. Oh, yes. Much better."

A hush fell on the room just then, as the guest of honor stepped through the raised entrance and paused at the top of the wide staircase. On one arm, an older man stood, the Duke her father. On the other, her mother.

The major domo announced them, and applause broke out in the room.

Upon witnessing such a ceremonial spectacle, Tilde had to stifle the urge to giggle. When she covered her grin with her fan, Betsy narrowed her eyes at her in admonishment.

"I suppose I've been dwelling in the country too long." She leaned forward and whispered.

"You're incorrigible." But then the musicians took up their instruments and another, younger gentleman stepped forward to offer Lady Elaine his arm. Dressed mostly in black, the man moved with a casual elegance. When he tilted his head to hear something his partner had said, a shiver ran down Tilde's spine. Did her eyes deceive her?

As the music struck up and he turned so that she caught a glimpse of his profile, she could see that indeed it was.

It was Jasper!

Her Jasper!

He was, indeed, the girl's father, and also the man she'd met eleven years before. She had not been mistaken.

"Isn't he handsome?" Betsy asked with a sigh. "And such a tragic figure. His wife passed away last year. She was the daughter of a duke as well. I suppose that, if first you don't succeed––"

"Try and try again." Tilde finished without thought. She ought not to be stunned.

All of the pieces began falling into place. When she'd known him, he'd begged her to call him Jasper. If he'd gone on to marry the daughter of a duke…

She shook her head. Of course, he was a peer.

She'd never stood a chance.

She swallowed hard. Althea and Eloise had lost their mother last year. Had they been close to her? Tilde, as a governess, knew more than anyone that some aristocratic families left the raising of their children to servants.

Her previous employers had not. They'd always made time for their daughters.

"They do make a lovely pair," Betsy whispered.

All eyes remained on the couple leading off the dance. Lady Elaine, so fresh and lovely… and so very young. Jasper, elegantly dressed, tall and oh so very handsome. Except he was far too old for the girl. Performing some mental math, she surmised he was practically twice the age of his dance partner.

He'd been twenty-four on the night he'd kissed her. She'd been seventeen. The same age Lady Elaine was now. So, yes, indeed. "He's more than twice her age!" Tilde could not help but exclaim to her sister.

"How do you know that? Besides, he's a man. Don't you remember when Lord Pemberton married Horatia Smythe? He was almost four times her age. He was a bent-over old man. The earl is most definitely not a bent-over old man."

"No." Tilde pinched her lips together. What was the matter with her?

"It would be quite scandalous if it were the other way around, though, wouldn't it?"

"Yes." This wasn't the first time Tilde had considered the disparities between gentlemen and ladies.

By now the dance was well underway and Jasper and Lady Elaine led the other couples with elegance and grace.

"He's an earl?" Tilde asked faintly.

"The Earl of… Worsby? Whorly? Oh, I can never remember them all. But I believe it starts with a 'W.' Or perhaps a 'V.'"

Tilde hadn't really known the man at all. One night. They'd spent fewer than three hours in one another's company. His attentions had never been serious. She'd thought it was magic whereas to him, she could not have been anything more than a handy bit of muslin for him to have some fun with.

She turned her back toward the dance floor. "I'm parched. Do you think there's some warm lemonade around here somewhere?"

Betsy seemed reluctant to lose their place.

"If we remain in this corner all night, no one will see your beautiful gowns."

Seeing the practicality in Tilde's reasoning, Betsy relented, and the girls picked their way around the edge of the dance floor. If no lemonade could be found, perhaps they could locate a few glasses of champagne.

She might as well enjoy herself tonight. If it was to be her last ball than she wasn't about to spend the evening fixating upon Lord Whateverhisnamewas.

An earl!

She removed two glasses from a passing waiter and handed one to Betsy.

"To us." She lifted the drink in mock salute.

And then, feeling more than a little reckless, threw back her head and swallowed the drink in one swallow.

An Earl, for heaven's sake!

CHAPTER 5

HE REMEMBERED

Hell and damnation, Jasper thought as he led the child onto the parquet dance floor. He would take his mother in hand tomorrow. She needed to know she could not organize his life. So many times, he'd given into her manipulations and demands so as not to embarrass her, but he could do so no longer.

Lady Elaine was lovely and graceful but oh, so very young.

Too young.

He faced her as the couples queued up. Judging by the length of the line behind them, he prepared to endure a dance that would surely last close to an hour. He'd much preferred to spend the evening at home. He already felt as though he'd abandoned his daughters for far too long.

Althea had cried when he stopped into the nursery to wish her goodnight. Eloise explained. "The nurse is mean. She makes Thea sit in the corner for not speaking up when addressed." Eloise had sounded so grown up. "And she takes away her doll."

Jasper clenched his teeth at the memory. He'd taken the woman aside and demanded she not punish Lady Althea for keeping quiet. He'd threatened to sack her if it happened again.

He was in no mood for a ball. Especially one so ridiculously extravagant. Grand for the sake of being grand, excessive and overstated merely because they could do so. The flowers clawed at him. The heat from the chandeliers already made the room stifling. God help him, they'd left the doors and windows closed in the hope that Prinny would stop by.

Prinny never stopped by.

Tomorrow, if the agency failed to present an acceptable candidate, perhaps he would advertise the post himself. Offer some incentive…

The girls needed a governess, and not just any governess.

He spun his partner and sauntered to the opposite end of the line almost without thinking. He'd probably performed this dance one hundred times.

Before Estelle had taken ill.

One tended to lose enthusiasm for any sort of celebration after watching a loved one die. He spun his neighbor's partner and then took Lady Elaine's gloved hand once again. The top of her head didn't quite meet his shoulders and her fingers felt thin and fragile in his hand.

Matilda Fortune's hand had not felt fragile. It had felt feminine, yes, but also strong and capable. And when she'd stood, she'd not had to tilt her head back far to meet his eyes.

Miss Fortune.

He wished he'd recognized her earlier. He'd have liked to ask her…

What? What would he have asked her?

Reaching up and leaning forward as other couples ducked under the long bridge of arms, the thought plagued him.

She had not married. She'd remained *Miss* Fortune. Nor had she had any child. Presumably.

What did she do with her time? Did she live in that small hamlet of a village? Perhaps she was a school teacher. She'd handled the girls with considerable ease. He suppressed a grin. She'd handled him firmly as well.

A spinster.

Or perhaps she had a paramour tucked away somewhere. Perhaps he'd not remembered her face, or her name immediately, but he'd always remembered the occasion of meeting her. As sad as the thought was, no other lady had affected him the same. Not his wife, and none of the ladies before her.

He and Miss Fortune, that night.

He'd not gone to Vauxhall looking for anything, or anyone. He'd simply found himself at loose ends when Lord Pike had mentioned the outing. Sitting in the tent, she'd not struck him as a beauty, by any means.

But she'd struck him, nonetheless.

And since no one had really known him there, he'd asked Pike to introduce him as Mr. Jasper Talbot. It had been refreshing to leave off the title for once.

He'd taken her walking and curiously wanted to know everything about her. Before no time at all, he'd ached to take her in his arms.

None of it had been based on logic or reason. It has simply been... attraction. The same as lightening to a tree––or to water. Had that been a once in a lifetime phenomenon? Would it be the same, if he were to touch her again? He shook his head, admonishing himself. He'd missed his opportunity to explore that attraction. Twice now.

He turned one last time and faced his partner as the music finally came to a halt.

As Lady Elaine stared up at him with stars in her eyes, he knew one thing for certain. No interest in this chit existed. If he were truly going to look for a wife, perhaps he'd best look amongst the adult ladies.

Bubbles of laughter rose up from a pair of women standing along the wall.

41

Familiar laughter.

Well, I'll be damned.

* * *

STANDING ALONE while Betsy danced with one of Aunt Nellies' friends' nephews, Tilde stared unseeing at other guests who seemed to be enjoying themselves immensely. Despite the champagne, and the lovely gown and the beautiful flowers all around her, Tilde wanted only to go home. Hopefully, Betsy and her aunt didn't intend staying for the duration of the evening. Tilde could laugh all night long, smile and make inane conversation, but none of it would take away the ironic sense of loss that had settled in her heart.

"You didn't mention you were travelling to London."

Tilde straightened her back at the masculine voice behind her. Gathering her wits, she slowly turned around.

Jasper.

"I didn't think you would be interested, *my lord.*"

When she'd left him last, he'd been overheated, irritated and worried about his two offspring. Tonight, he appeared cool and formal, dressed in almost all black, but for lace at his wrists and neck, both a pristine white.

His dark eyes flared with awareness.

He'd remembered.

Taking her hand in his, he bowed low as he chuckled. "Have you promised the next set to another already?"

Of course, she had not. And for the moment, her mind went blank. She'd been aware of him all evening but had honestly not expected him to offer even a nod, let alone ask for a dance.

"But it's a waltz," she finally managed.

"Do you not waltz? Or is it that you disapprove of the dance in particular?" A challenging glint lit his gaze. Despite their first meeting having occurred nearly eleven years earlier, she supposed it would have been quite hypocritical of her to disapprove.

"I can perform the dance adequately." As a governess, one tended to participate in more dance lessons than one's actual students. She lifted her chin, "and I find no fault in it whatsoever."

But she found fault in him. It annoyed her that his appeal was not diminished even though she'd come to learn he'd only been toying with her on that night long ago.

Did he intend to toy with her again?

Or was he simply being courteous?

"Do you not wish to dance? Would you prefer to take a turn about the room with me instead?"

So, he intended to talk.

"The next set has not been reserved." At his raised brows, she added, "I wish to dance."

A grin tugged at Jasper's lips, but he held out his arm. "Then dance, you shall."

And then he led Tilde to the middle of the floor. As they passed a cluster of more well-to-do guests, Tilde thought she saw somebody point her out, and then whisper something uncharitable.

They were not admiring her dress.

She straightened her back and did her best to ignore them.

And then things became awkward.

Standing in the middle of the floor, she turned to face him. Based upon what the other couples were doing, they would be expected to hold one another.

It was quite apparent that Jasper experienced none of the unease that she was.

Nonplussed, he took hold of her right hand and placed his other at her waist.

She'd been kissed several times over the past decade... well...

43

four times, to be exact. And she'd danced the waltz with at least six different instructors.

So why did she feel like a clumsy girl of ten and seven again?

"I apologize for not remembering you last week." His gaze settled on her intently. "You felt familiar––you *looked* familiar to me. I can only beg forgiveness. And offer that my mind was quite befuddled by my daughters' antics."

Thank Heavens an immediate response was not required just then, as the quartet lifted their bows and began playing.

She'd learned how to use the balls of her feet and rise and fall with the steps, to move her shoulders smoothly and parallel with the floor. She knew to allow her partner to steer her. The dance itself came almost effortlessly.

But… She stared into eyes as black as the sea at night and fought the sensations rising up from her past.

"Will you?" His voice was the same, only deeper, more cultured.

Would she? "There's nothing to forgive." She forced her lips into a cool smile.

The music flowed like water while she floated on air. *Your first kiss holds the answer to all that you desire.*

"Are your parents here in London as well?" His question, such an innocent one.

"They passed some time ago." But the loss is always in my heart, she wanted to say to him. Again, she felt that she'd known him forever. That he'd understand who she was without her having to explain…

The look he sent her was sympathetic. "I'm sorry."

Or perhaps he did not understand. He didn't even know her. He never had.

"Their carriage turned over on the road to Brighton." She would tell him something of it. "The day after I met you, as a matter of fact."

He missed a step and they both stumbled to recover.

Enough Tilde! Leave it in the past.

"And not that it matters," she added, ignoring her own inclination. "But I would have told you, had you come."

"May I call upon you tomorrow?" He'd whispered the words when they had broken apart from one another in order to catch their breath. She had nodded, unable to speak.

"It was a long time ago." She'd make the excuse for him. "And you were young. As was I." But at the time she'd believed in magic.

He cleared his throat. She'd made him uncomfortable.

"I can only beg your forgiveness."

He raised their arms and twirled her effortlessly, bringing a surprising gasp of laughter to her throat.

"That's twice you need to be forgiven, then? Am I correct?" It made sense for her to be lighthearted about this. They were dancing for Heaven's sake. The time to question him would have been over a decade ago.

Not here in a ballroom, when anyone could overhear…

"Why did you not come?" As much as she would have liked to recall the question to her lips, a part of her needed to hear it. Knowing he was nobody special after all might put an end to any regrets she had about gentlemen in general.

About wondering if she ought to have flirted more? Compromised some of herself in an attempt to pursue love…

He grimaced. "I was a stupid young fool?"

She couldn't help but smile at that. She'd appropriated far too much significance into their meeting than she ought to have.

"I was quite naïve, myself," she admitted. But she could tell she'd made him feel guilty.

"If it matters, my memory of your name, and your face faded, but I never forgot that evening. And after seeing you again, it all came back to me."

Ah, but that arrow landed sharply. Why could he not have left it at his stupid young foolishness?

"I took advantage of your naivete. I owed you an offer."

But she was shaking her head. "Only if we'd been caught."

Such an offer never would have stuck. He'd gone on to marry the daughter of a duke. The night had been a frivolous one. Her parents had barely lurked within the circle of genteel society. "And you oughtn't remind me of my own bad behavior." Heat suffused her cheeks upon making such an admission.

Throughout their conversation, as they danced, they'd been staring into one another's eyes.

It had not been uncomfortable. It had not felt improper.

"I was the one who behaved poorly." His smiled disarmed her, just as it had before. "You, my dear Miss Fortune, acted with all required discretion."

This time she allowed her laughter to escape.

"Are all youths so foolish?" She tilted her head as she asked the question. Having this conversation with him, although bitter-sweet, lent her a sophistication she didn't own. Dismissing her once true love. Laughing at the foolishness of both their youths.

He didn't answer right away.

"I would hope not." And then that tender rueful smile.

Oh, but he had a way. One minute she believed him to be shallow and unfeeling, and the next he reminded her of the man she'd made him out to be in her dreams––a fantasy lover––too good to be true.

"Are your daughters enjoying London?" She needed to change the subject to something less personal.

In doing so, she managed to summon deep creases in his forehead as well as a most discouraging scowl.

"They are… adjusting."

He seemed to not wish to discuss the subject. It was sad really. And disappointing. A father ought to be happy to discuss two such lovely girls as he was lucky enough to have.

Perhaps it had something to do with his recent loss.

"I'm sorry to hear of your wife's passing." That was a sentiment anyone would say, was it not? She could not come right out and ask him if he'd been betrothed already on the night they'd kissed at Vauxhall.

Could she?

"How long had you been married?"

He shook his head at her. "I was not engaged when you and I met." Oh, but it was happening again. That feeling of knowing, of familiarity and... just knowing. "But we had been married just over ten years."

That was a very long time. And he'd come away with two lovely daughters.

She hoped he'd had love in his marriage. It was sad to lose a loved one, but ten years of unhappiness would have been, perhaps, even sadder.

Of course, he might disagree with such a sentiment if she allowed herself to utter it.

She pinched her lips together tightly, having already spoken out of turn.

"I loved her." He answered her unasked question. "Marriage can be a difficult endeavor, though."

And then he shook his head, wincing, as though he too, had said more than he'd wished.

She needed another subject. This conversation was becoming all too personal. "Are you going to ask for Lady Elaine? Everyone is speculating, you know."

He nearly winced. She could tell by the twitch of his lip before he shuttered his emotions. "My mother is good friends with the duchess."

That was no answer at all.

Tilde held her tongue again, and staring beyond his shoulders and out the door, took on the ennui she'd watched on so many other women's faces that evening. "Lovely weather we've been having."

When she returned her gaze to his eyes, he'd narrowed them at her. "I'm not going to ask for Lady Elaine, she's a child."

Tilde laughed and then bit her bottom lip.

"I'm aware she is the same age you were when we met."

Tilde laughed again. "You remembered my age?"

At that he rolled his eyes. If either of them had been paying attention, they'd have realize several onlookers watched them curiously.

"Of course. I was a stupid young fool, but I was quite enamored with you that evening." And simple as that, he set her heart racing again.

"And you were four and twenty." She uttered the words without thinking.

Their feet stopped moving as the music drew to a close. Two more dances in this set. Could she make it through them without breaking into tears?

CHAPTER 6

SECOND TIME AROUND

*W*illoughby kept silent as the second dance of the set began.

She'd asked him why he'd not come to see her the next morning. He remembered planning on it. He remembered thinking he'd buy her flowers. Something bright and big.

Why hadn't he gone?

And out of the corner of his eyes he met his mother's steely gaze watching him from her vantage point beside the Duchess of Marvelle.

Hell and damnation. Yes. His mother had stopped him that morning. She'd asked after his destination and he'd told her. She'd wrinkled her nose when he'd mentioned who Matilda's parents were.

"You oughtn't visit her so soon. You're apt to give rise to expectations that you'll never meet." She'd advised. "Furthermore, I have need of an escort…"

He'd had every intention of making a call to Miss Fortune's home the following day…

He'd accompanied his mother to Estelle's parents garden party instead.

He vaguely remembered hearing of a couple being killed on their way to Brighton but hadn't realized they had been Matilda's parents.

Would he have made the time to go to her had he realized? He'd lain in bed recalling how he'd felt to touch her. His recollections had perhaps not been as innocent as hers. He'd remembered her eager kisses, her fingers threading through his hair, down his neck...

"It was a most memorable evening," he admitted aloud.

She'd been staring off over his shoulder, as lost in thought as he had been, but upon hearing his words, slid her glance back to his face.

"I think that perhaps, not everyone is so lucky." Her smile wound itself around his chest.

It was what he'd thought before, in the carriage, when he'd first remembered.

"A very special moment in time," he agreed.

He pulled her slightly closer. Not so much as to raise eyebrows but because...

He did not know why.

He'd not intended to dance with her. He'd asked impulsively, as soon as he'd realized the set was to be a waltz. And he'd not intended to tell her so much of his memories.

The two of them had been ill fated. Jasper maneuvered them around a cluster of couples near the edge of the floor.

Now wasn't the time to lose himself in recollections of the past.

The last governess would be coming tomorrow and hopefully he could approve of her. He might even return to Warwick Creek ahead of schedule. He wasn't prepared to negotiate the bait and subsequent traps he'd inevitably come upon in town. Melancholy made him careless. If he wasn't watchful, he'd find himself leg-shackled to a wide-eyed debutante and his mother would be turning the key.

"You're troubled."

Her words floated up like a pleasant scent.

"And there you have it. The third time I must beg your forgiveness."

She did not laugh this time, at his self-deprecating comment. Rather she watched him with those eyes of hers. "Hazel." He stared into them. "And tonight, they appear more green than brown."

She didn't fall for his change of subject.

"Your girls will be fine."

And they would be. If only… "Althea hardly talks at all. I fear Eloise removes all incentive."

"They are five? Six? And they've lost their mother." Her voice sounded with some authority. "But they have their father. And one another. I remember how close my sisters and I became after my parents passing. And we had my aunt. Children are resilient Jas– my lord."

"One never ceases to worry." He admitted. "But I find some comfort in your words."

A sad smile tipped up her lips. "I'm glad."

"But you never gave me what I asked." She tilted her head questioningly. "Will you grant me your forgiveness, please, Miss Fortune?"

That sad smile stretched into something more comforting. "Of course. How could I not?"

And once again the music slowed to a halt. One more dance in the set, and then he'd bid her farewell. They could go their separate ways and with no regrets to muddy their magical memory. He did not relinquish his hold on her as they awaited the next song. And then he flicked his glance to the terrace.

"Would you care to take a turn in the garden?"

CHAPTER 7

SHE'D WONDERED

*W*ithout warning, the urge to make an escape became all too powerful for Jasper to ignore. It must be the overwhelming scent of the flower arrangements, combined with all the ladies' perfumes.

And the heat. Both from perspiring bodies and hundreds of burning candles.

Because he didn't wait for Miss Fortune to answer, taking her by the arm instead, and practically dragging her off the shining floor.

Cool air hit him immediately as he opened the door.

"But my sister––" She began to protest with only the slightest resistance. Then she seemed to change her mind and closed the door behind them.

A handful of gentlemen stood near the edged pavement, smoking cigars and chatting. Jasper recognized most of them. They were escaping their wives and the banal conversations inside.

He acknowledged them with a curt nod but then turned in the opposite direction. He had no wish to introduce Matilda Fortune to them in that moment.

He was whisking a young woman away from the protection of the ballroom. He wanted to be alone with her.

Best no one know her identity.

Once out of earshot he exhaled a relieved sigh. "I'm not ready for any of this." Had he really admitted that out loud?

She reached up with her free hand and squeezed his wrist. He appreciated that she didn't deign to offer encouragement, or probe as to why. Instead, his words simply hung in the air for both of them to examine. He hated how self–pitying they sounded.

As the path narrowed, he drew her closer so she wouldn't be scratched by encroaching branches.

"After Mama and Papa's funerals, I tried to go on with my life as though nothing had changed, as though their death was just another obstacle for me to get over… And it seemed to work for a while. I threw myself into my schooling and admonished Betsy and Chloe for failing to do likewise.

"What I failed to realize was that *my* refusal to grieve created an even greater pain for them. When I came home from school for the holidays, the magnitude of our loss finally hit home. We sat down to dine, my sisters and my aunt. And I turned to the head of the table where my father had always sat… And he wasn't there."

"It was Christmas and my Mama and Papa would not be a part of it." She made a small laughing sound as though to dismiss her sentimentality. "It was the first time I'd cried since their death. And then Betsy broke down, and Chloe… and poor little Charlotte. She was practically still a baby."

"With our tears, though, we realized we had one another. It was a horrid Christmas, but as long as we had each other, we could endure almost anything…" Another disparaging laugh. "I'm sorry to go on so… My point is… You lost your wife. You mustn't force yourself to move on if you aren't yet prepared."

Jasper contemplated her sad tale. Was it possible he yet grieved for Estelle?

He and Miss Fortune had been walking toward the center of the garden and the sounds of gushing water grew louder as they approached the large fountain. The moon reflected off the rippling pool and a gentle breeze stirred the leaves and branches like a gentle caress.

The setting could not have been more romantic in any way.

Miss Fortune dropped his arm and stepped forward to gaze up at the cascading spray.

He couldn't help but study her closely, hoping to understand what about this woman attracted him so.

Her chestnut hair had been styled in a flattering manner, and her gown showed off her rounded figure to advantage.

"Tell me something of your life." He wanted to know more about her. In many ways, she was practically a complete stranger to him. "Is your home in Rotter's Corner?"

"Excuse me?" She'd glanced back at him with raised eyebrows.

"The village, where the festival…"

"Oh, Heaven's no! I was simply travelling through… the same as you."

And then their eyes held, almost as though they were both imagining the same thing: That but for such an ironic twist of fate, they might never have become reacquainted. They might have been lost to one another forever…

The secret to finding your future lies in the fortune you lost in your past. Madame Zeta's words stole their way into his mind.

Folly. Ridiculousness. And yet…

"My aunt lives here, in London. I'm between positions and it seemed as good a time as any to come home for a visit." Her face glowed and her gaze seemed to soften as she spoke of her family.

His gaze fell on her lips. She was doing it again… mesmerizing him.

And like a moth to the flame, he couldn't help but step closer, not quite touching, but if he reached out…

She did not step away from him.

"Your aunt lives in Mayfair?"

"Number thirty-six Wigmore Street." She spoke the address as though reciting it for school, and then laughed. He rather enjoyed the sound. It wasn't an annoying titter, feigned for deliberate effect, but a melodic expression of mirth.

He couldn't help but match her grin. "Number twelve Brooks."

He'd returned to London many times and she'd resided within less than a mile of his townhome. A strand of her hair caught on her lips and he lifted his hand to brush it away.

At his touch, she blushed and dropped her head, then turned back to stare into the fountain. "Will you remain in London for the season?" Her voice came out sounding wistful.

He did not know. In that moment, all he knew was that he wanted to pull her up against him. Taste her lips again.

That enchanted feeling had not been real, it couldn't have been, and yet some defiant need demanded he find out.

"Matilda." His voice came out gravelly sounding. He cleared his throat. She turned to face him.

Her chin lifted and she gazed back at him boldly. Did she wonder as well?

When he'd kissed her before, he remembered, he'd braced his hands above her on the bark of the tree. This time he wound them around her waist, drawing her close.

She exhaled sharply, still gazing into his eyes.

She wondered too. He knew it.

She was not a stranger to him. After all these years. He didn't know how, or why. But…

He knew her.

She trembled beneath his hands and the pulse in her neck fluttered like a trapped butterfly.

When her lashes dropped, he swept in and claimed her lips.

* * *

SHE'D WONDERED.

When he'd led her onto the terrace, she'd known this would happen. And she'd given in to him––to it.

Because she'd wondered.

From the moment he took her hand to assist her out of that blasted tent.

She'd wondered.

When he'd placed her hand in his and led her around the dance floor.

She'd wondered.

But now, a roaring filled her ears, lights flashed behind her eyes, and she melted her body into his. He tasted just as magical as before. She had not imagined it—the excitement, the effervescent wonder, the building need as heat coursed to her center.

None of it was familiar and yet a part of her was convinced she'd finally come home.

He turned his head and delved his mouth deeper into hers.

Jasper.

The urge to rejoice warred with an equally strong urge to weep. But she did neither, choosing instead to wind her arms around his neck and cling for all that she was worth.

Because she knew how this would turn out––the same as it had before. It would end. She would return to her world, and he to his. And she'd never feel these emotions again. Because these were once in a lifetime sensations.

Willing time to stand still, she pushed all thought away and without any hesitation, kissed him back.

And kissed him some more.

He adjusted his stance, spreading his legs wide so that their faces were level with one another. His hands drifted curiously up and down her back, eventually coming to rest upon the flare of her buttocks.

His hold tightened and she met him with equal force.

If not for a distant burst of raucous laughter, the moment might never have ended.

But of course, it did.

He lifted his head and glanced around. She buried her face against his chest.

After taking a moment to catch his breath, Jasper was the one to break the silence.

"It seems I lose all manner of discretion when it comes to you, yet again."

He sounded apologetic, but matter of fact.

Tilde nodded and drawing on willpower she'd completely relinquished this evening, she gently, but firmly, pushed him away.

"It seems... ah... there is something... extraordinary..." Oh, Heavens, but she was making a ninny of herself. "Of course, it cannot be all that extraordinary..." Would he contradict her?

Silence met her statement. When she deigned to look up at him, he was scrubbing one hand down his face.

"It's quite inexplicable, really." She added. And then the thought struck her that he mightn't have experienced their kiss quite the same as she had. She hesitantly took another step backward, placing more space between them. She bit her lip and winced.

But he was shaking his head. "Will you throw your slippers at me if I beg forgiveness yet again? That must be a record, four times in less than one hour."

Had it only been one hour since he'd appeared to request a dance? Was it possible for a person's life to be turned upside down so quickly?

Her heart yet raced and she clasped her hands together to keep them from shaking.

"Shall we return inside?" Her voice wasn't trembling, and she supposed that was a good thing. "My sister will be wondering..."

"But of course." He started but then paused and reached out to touch her hair. "This braid is coming unpinned." He winced. "There are quite a few actually."

A low moan escaped Tilde's lips before she could stop it. She could not afford to draw scandal, as low as she was. Employers did not appreciate governesses who were immersed in public disgrace.

"Hold still. Did you forget I just spent almost a full week travelling in a carriage with my twin five-year-old daughters? Without a nanny or governess?" He was winding and twisting her hair, removing pins and replacing them.

Betsy would know it was different, but no one else would.

"I didn't think of that." She murmured, enjoying the feel of his hands in her hair despite herself.

"You mentioned you were between posts. When does your new one begin?" He moved to the back of her head and went to adjusting another braid.

"The Stanhope agency has an interview lined up for me tomorrow morning." His fingers faltered and then went back to work.

"You're a... governess then?"

"I am," she answered. "The girls I'd been caring for are too old to require a governess any longer. I was sad to leave them, but it's quite satisfying employment."

He made something of a choking sound and then inserted one last pin.

CHAPTER 8

THE INTERVIEW

*T*ilde stared at the address and furrowed her brows.

Number twelve Brooks. It seemed familiar somehow. Perhaps because it wasn't very far from her aunt's townhouse. The sun shone so bright and cheerful that she wouldn't even hire a hackney.

Peaches would enjoy the walk.

Leaving her dog with Aunt Nellie was not an option, so she'd be upfront with whoever considered her services. If they wanted her expertise in raising and teaching their children, they'd make accommodations for her pet as well.

She knew from experience, that an employer could do far worse. Furthermore, any family that wouldn't welcome a sweet baby like Peaches wasn't a family she'd wish to live with.

Because a governess didn't merely work for her employer. She spent practically every waking hour with them.

Therefore, their approval of her pet was even more of an important consideration than their approval of her.

Of which, considering the numerous ladies who'd made attempts to steal her from the Brightly's, she didn't doubt for a moment.

The agency had sent a note around the day before stating that, upon approval, this employer would wish that she take up the position immediately. Tilde assumed that she would likely be leaving London. Most wealthy families didn't relish having their offspring underfoot in the midst of the Season.

She hoped the children weren't too young… nor too old. She preferred taking on girls who were over the age of four but not past the age of four and ten. Boys, in her experience anyhow, tended to be more difficult to manage.

Not that she wasn't up to the task.

So caught up in her thoughts she was––that had not been centered around Jasper––that she nearly passed her destination. She allowed Peaches to relieve herself on a patch of grass before approaching the door and lifting the heavy knocker that had been shaped into a rather impressive 'W'.

Number twelve. Again, something niggled.

The butler opened the door and with a sniff, stared down his rather long nose at her. "Miss Fortune, I presume?"

"Ah, yes. I'm here to interview," she glanced down at the missive she carried. "A Lord Willoughby."

The butler took note of Peaches and scowled. "Are you certain, madam?"

"The agency sent me over. I understand the family is in need of a governess." The butler's frown deepened and so she added, "My dog assists in all my duties. She is quite essential."

Another sniff.

"Unless Lord Willoughby objects." She went to step backward but he halted her with a wince.

"No. Please. This way please. I'll inform the earl that you've arrived." If the butler's demeanor was anything to go by, it was quite possible that she was wasting her time.

Nonetheless, she and Peaches followed the butler. When he went to climb the long staircase, Tilde scooped Peaches into her arms. With such short legs, her pup would have required at least an hour to make the climb.

Upon reaching the top, Tilde's eyes were drawn to the paintings hung all along the corridor. His lordships ancestors, no doubt. But then.

She stopped at one of them and tilted her head.

It could not be.

"Miss Fortune." His voice rumbled from behind her, causing her to jump and invoking a sharp bark from Peaches. Peaches hardly ever barked, only when in this man's company apparently.

As she turned to confirm her suspicions, she found herself dismayed, pleased, confused... and…

Disappointed.

She'd have to ask the agency to find her another position.

He'd been dressed in immaculate evening clothes the night before. Today he wore riding breeches and looked as though he'd already been out for some exercise.

She stood filled with ironic astonishment, he seemed utterly at ease.

"Did you know?"

When he didn't answer, she twisted her head to look for someone else. Perhaps he was merely a guest in the household. Or a figment of her imagination even…

The disapproving butler had disappeared however, leaving them standing in the corridor alone… except for Peaches of course.

When she settled her gaze on him once again, he shrugged.

"I hadn't a clue until you mentioned the agency. I didn't even know you were a governess, although I should have." He then gestured a hand toward a pair of open doors. "Shall we?"

Oh, good heavens. He didn't expect her to go through with the interview, did he?

"I–" She didn't move from where she stood. "Um." Oh, this was horrible. "There's been a mistake."

61

He smiled in a manner she could only consider to be slightly patronizing. "You are here for the interview, are you not?"

She stepped tentatively toward the staircase, clutching Peaches to her chest. Just last night she'd been locked in a most passionate embrace, a most inappropriate one, and today...

"I cannot have you for an employer." Surely, he must realize this.

"But you are in need of a position, are you not?" Was he joking?

"I am, but−−"

"And I am in desperate need of a governess. You told me so yourself, on two separate occasions, I believe."

"Of course, but−−"

"Are you unwilling to take my daughters on?"

"Of course not!"

"Then won't you at least come inside and discuss it?" Those black eyes of his seemed almost to be pleading with her. But she just shook her head.

"I cannot−−"

"It's Miss Fortune! From the festival!" A childish voice called out in excitement.

"Peaches!" A second, softer but no less enthusiastic declaration followed. And before Tilde could make her escape, two bundles of energy dressed in baby blue frocks burst upon them from behind two large plants.

They might have knocked her over had their father not reached out and effortlessly swooped them up, each under one arm.

"Papa! Is she going to be our new governess? You said you were meeting with the new governess this morning!"

That would be Eloise, Tilde remembered, watching the girl squirming in her father's grasp. Although considerably more subdued, Althea was all smiles, her gaze fixed on Tilde's dog.

Peaches was no help at all, tail wagging and tongue hanging out enthusiastically.

"Girls!" He made every attempt to sound disapproving but the laughter in his eyes belied it. "Why aren't you in the nursery?"

"You said you were going to hire our governess this morning. Thea and I need to get a look at her so we could tell you if she is a good one or not."

Althea simply nodded in agreement.

Tilde's heart dropped into her shoes. She needed to capture control of this situation, somehow.

Still holding Peaches, she placed the toe of her right foot behind her and dipped slightly. "I must admit, I've never curtseyed to two ladies hanging upside down before."

"It's because Papa has taken us in hand."

Althea giggled.

Tilde raised her gaze to Jasper's––Lord Willoughby's face. Oh, but it would be impossible to live in his home, care for his children… as his employee.

"Won't you come inside and sit down." He winced as he glanced at the two imps he'd caught up. "Please?" he added.

Oh heavens, how could she not? She only nodded.

He lowered the girls onto their feet and with the most unconvincing disapproval, ordered them back to the nursery. Eloise turned to leave immediately but Althea tugged at her father and pointed toward Peaches.

Appearing only minutely apologetic, he took hold of his daughter's hand and rose to his full height. "I believe that Althea wonders if she might say hello to Peaches before taking her leave."

Tiny arrows pierced Tilde's heart. "But of course."

Dropping to the carpeted floor, Tilde lowered Peaches so she could stand on her little legs.

"Do you remember me?" The little girl's wide eyes appeared concerned.

Tilde was aware that her sister watched from a few feet away.

"I am certain Peaches remembers you." Tilde reached out, clasped Althea's hand in hers, and drew her gently forward. "Do you remember how she likes to be petted?"

The dark little head nodded and in a matter of seconds, she was petting and cooing at Tilde's small companion. Peaches responded by licking the child's hand, and occasionally the bottom of her chin.

Althea turned to look over her shoulder. "Licks are kisses. Aren't they, Peaches?"

Tilde could only nod. Yes. Those licks, indeed, were kisses. When she glanced up at Jasper, she thought perhaps his eyes glistened ever so slightly.

He cleared his throat. "Thank Miss Fortune. Althea, off to the nursery with you both."

The little girl kissed Peaches on top of her head, and then rose reluctantly. Rather than say anymore, she dipped into a curtsey and then backed up.

"I'm sorry, my lord." A stern looking middle aged woman stood in the doorway. "I left the nursery for a moment…" Ah, the woman had lost track of her charges. She threw a sour glance in the direction of the twins and then a repentant one toward Lord Willoughby.

"You'll be more diligent in the future Mrs. Crabtree." His jaw tightened and his eyes turned cold. He seemed disinclined to assuage any guilt the woman experienced. Tilde had never seen this side of him, in the… six or so hours they'd spent together over the past eleven years.

Her heart would shrivel up and die if he ever looked at her that way.

"Good day, Lady Althea, Lady Eloise." If Jasper was an earl, then that meant the girls were officially ladies. "Thank you for such a warm greeting."

Lady Eloise clung to the door frame. "You will be our

governess, won't you?"

Tilde swallowed hard. "We'll see. Even if I am not, you are more than welcome to visit me while I'm in London." With a glance toward Lady Althea, she added, "and Peaches, of course."

The sour nursemaid then ushered Lord Willoughby's daughters away, closing the door behind her.

"Now." He let out an exasperated sigh. "Won't you take your seat again?"

A web of need from those tiny girls wound around her. Staring at him, Tilde did not move, because she felt his need as well.

He likely did not realize it. And he'd deny any such possibility, but Tilde knew how this would all play out.

He would rely upon Tilde to manage the children and perhaps to comfort him as well. She would be available at his leisure and both of them might perhaps even succumb to physical passion.

And that would be all.

Because she would never be his equal.

And knowing her heart had already engaged somewhat, she wasn't willing to expose it to the inevitable trouncing it would take.

* * *

JASPER COULD NOT HAVE BEEN MORE pleased. She'd captured the girls' hearts. She had a way about her... rational yet gentle and compassionate. She demanded a certain respect but always with a twist of humor. Miss Matilda Fortune would be perfect for his children.

He dared not ponder how perfectly she'd fit in his arms the night before. Nor how perfect her lips had tasted.

No, he must consider his daughters' needs first and foremost. He must hire Miss Fortune to be their governess.

Unfortunately, she appeared as though she was of quite a

different mindset. She'd scooped her dog up and was backing purposefully toward the door.

"Please. Stay." It wasn't often that one refused to do his bidding.

Other than his mother, of course.

And then there were his daughters…

But she was shaking her head. "I cannot. You must understand…"

Without thinking, he stepped forward and grasped her by the arm. He needed her.

For the girls, of course.

The moment he touched her, though, he understood her refusal. Because the instant his hand grasped her arm, he found it difficult to stop at that. An overwhelming desire to dig his fingers into her upswept hair, tilt her head back and plunder her mouth, was nearly too much to overcome.

He released her, as though burned.

"Of course, what was I thinking? I'm sorry." He could not hire a woman–– one that he wanted for himself––to be given charge of his daughters.

Nonetheless, she paused in her retreat.

"Will you tell them… that I am sorry. And that I would love to be their governess but… it just didn't work out."

Jasper clasped his own hands behind his back and stepped over to stare out the window, lest he act unforgivably with this woman for the millionth time since they'd become acquainted. "Althea doesn't talk." He glanced over his shoulder at her. "She hasn't said more than twenty words since her mother's death."

TILDE FURROWED HER BROWS. "BUT?" The child had talked to her. And then she pondered that thought.

The child had not talked to her. *She'd talked to Peaches.*

Jasper was nodding. "You see. I would not ask you to stay here for me. But because I fear my daughter requires something special." A small, ironic chuckle. "And that something special seems to be your dog."

Tilde blinked. Oh, but this raised the stakes indeed.

It would seem the height of selfishness to refuse to help a sad and lost little girl. And worst of all, Tilde had guessed as much. She'd known Lady Althea required gentle persuasion. But to hear Jasper put her need so plainly crumbled her objections.

Tilde absentmindedly lowered Peaches to the carpet and began pacing the room.

After crossing back and forth three times she stopped, tapped her finger against her lips and addressed him. "She speaks with Lady Eloise." This was not a question. "Not to you?"

He continued staring out the window. "No."

Tilde felt confident that she could draw the child's personality out--calm many of her fears. Althea quite obviously was capable of talking. It would simply be a matter of gaining her trust.

Could she and Lord Willoughby set aside this... magic? No. She would cease to call it any such nonsense. Passion? Chaos? Whatever it was, could they ignore it?

For the sake of the child.

"I may, perhaps, have led you to believe that I'm a certain type of lady, by my actions on two of the occasions we met." She cleared her throat. "But now, at the risk of sounding hypocritical, I must adamantly insist that I am not that certain type of lady at all... and I do not intend to ever become such."

He cleared his throat. "I hold your character in the highest esteem, Miss Fortune."

She met his gaze, narrowing her eyes at him. "And regardless of certain..." She raised her hand and rubbed her fingers together as she searched for the proper word.

"Inclinations?" He supplied helpfully.

"Yes." When she nodded in appreciation, she surmised that his eyes could appear nearly black but also a smoky gray. What had she been saying? Oh yes… "Regardless of these inclinations, if, and that is a very big if, I were to accept the position, I would expect that we never entertain those…"

"Inclinations."

"Exactly."

"Because you shall be in my employ." He supplied. "And a certain degree of professionalism must be maintained. Of course, you'll wish to keep me appraised of the girls progress and any difficulties you might be experiencing with them."

"Indeed." She agreed. "And I've always insisted upon an open-door policy with my employers in order to be an effective governess. I realize this may be a tad unconventional, but I am not the most conventional of governesses. What good does it do for me to raise them up if the result is that they know nothing of their own parents? Or parent, as the case may be."

He watched her slyly. "What good does it do indeed?"

"Is that a dog? In my house?" An older woman with silver hair piled high on her head and dressed in elegant finery had entered the room unnoticed. With a disapproving frown she raised one hand to her chest, revealing heavy rings upon her gnarled fingers, and glowered down at Peaches. Unfortunately, the woman unadvisedly bent over and began shaking one of those fingers admonishingly at Tilde's rather sensitive little pooch. "Outside, now! Who gave permission for this mongrel--"

Peaches, a most submissive animal, did not require angry reprimands. Ever. And if someone deigned to speak harshly to the pup…

"You may not want to do that–"

But it was too late. Shivering, Peaches had already bent her back legs and was squatting purposefully on what appeared to be a valuable Persian rug.

Had appeared to be a valuable Persian rug, that was. Tilde was not too certain such an artifact would survive the thorough cleaning it now required.

Tilde shrugged. If the woman chose to treat an animal thusly, well then…?

Lord Willoughby cleared his throat. "Miss Fortune, may I present my mother, the Dowager Countess of Willoughby. Mother, this is Miss Fortune. And I believe," he turned a questioning glance toward Tilde. "Althea and Eloise's new governess."

If possible, her ladyship's frown deepened even more.

Ignoring Tilde's curtsey, Lady Willoughby pursed her lips. "I told you that Lady Birchenbich was willing enough to send her former help over. Is this really necessary? And a dog? Really Willoughby? The mongrel just ruined a carpet that's been in the family for over three centuries."

Jasper ran one hand through his hair and then proceeded to scrub it down his face. "I believe Miss Fortune can help Althea–"

"Oh posh! Nothing a little discipline cannot resolve."

Tilde straightened her spine. This woman was Jasper's *mother*. She was the twin's *grandmother*.

"And I refuse to allow a dog in my house. I'm afraid Miss Fortune here is going to have to remove him at once."

"Peaches is a lady." Tilde inserted.

Jasper's mother whirled her face around to glare daggers at Tilde.

And then she turned to Jasper once again.

But he was having none of his mother's objections. "I'm afraid the decision has been made, and might I remind you mother, that this is my home? Althea responds well to the dog. Peaches is going to be a welcome addition to our household."

"The dog?" Lady Willoughby's eyes widened in horror.

"As will Miss Fortune."

A tense silence settled on the room and then his mother, apparently coming to a decision, withdrew her claws.

"Of course, it is your home, darling." Lady Willoughby said in a sickly-sweet tone. "If you wish the dog to remain, we'll make him most welcome." And then she wrinkled her brow, as though remembering something.

She turned back to finally address Tilde. "Miss Fortune? You say? I believe I knew your parents. Didn't they die under suspicious circumstances a few years back?" She stretched thin lips into a tight smile that Tilde mistrusted immediately.

Tilde's parents, although members of the ton, had not exactly mingled with the highest sticklers. "They died in a carriage accident, eleven years ago, my lady."

Lady Willoughby waved one hand in the air. "One must always speak kindly of the dead, mustn't one?"

"Lucky for you." Tilde answered beneath her breath.

"Pardon me?"

Tilde had always been able to find something redeeming in even the most disagreeable of individuals… but in this instance, such a feat might prove to be impossible. Lady Willoughby didn't so much seem to show affection for her son but a desire to control him. And she showed no evidence of any fondness or warmth for her granddaughters.

Without answering, Tilde scooped Peaches off the dampened carpet and turned toward Lord Willoughby.

Not Jasper.

Not her first kiss.

But toward the man who was soon to be her employer. "When would you like me to start?"

"Would tomorrow be asking too much?" He winced at his own request. "As you've told me on more than one occasion…"

Yes. The twins' need for a governess had grown quite dire.

"I shall arrive promptly at eight in the morning." She was going to do this. "You and I can lay out the terms of this agreement before I officially begin my duties. If you are amenable to a meeting, then?"

Lady Willoughby appeared horrified but Jas– *Lord Willoughby* appeared quite satisfied with himself.

She'd see if he remained so tomorrow. Because terms must be agreed upon and put in writing. An independent woman had only herself to protect her circumstances.

"Good day, Lord Willoughby. Lady Willoughby."

Lady Willoughby only sniffed.

Jasper smiled.

What had Tilde gotten herself into?

CHAPTER 9

NO MORE RELAPSES

"*Y*ou're going to work for the Earl of Willoughby?" Betsy studied Tilde skeptically in between stitching together one of her newest creations. Unbeknownst to Tilde, three different ladies had approached Betsy regarding the two dresses. They'd recognized a unique style and had wondered if the gowns had been sewn by a French dressmaker.

It seemed they were interested in commissioning gowns for themselves.

"I begin tomorrow." She inserted.

"Is that why he sought you out then?" Betsy's brows furrowed.

Tilde couldn't lie to Betsy. They'd always been closest in age as well as temperament. "We have a prior acquaintance."

This caused Betsy to set her needle aside and give Tilde her full attention. "Did you meet him while working for Lady Brightly?"

"Before that. Eleven years ago." And then it all came tumbling out. "And it was much more than a prior acquaintance. He's the first man who ever kissed me. At Vauxhall just before Mama and Papa's accident. And obviously, it never amounted to anything...

But then we happened upon one another at a small village fair outside of London last week. And he kissed me again last night. And... he's going to be my employer. I fear it's going to be difficult... His mother, Lady Willoughby is atrocious, but his daughters are the sweetest children imaginable, and *they need me!* I'm to begin tomorrow." It felt good to tell Betsy all of this. Her sister would be quite forthcoming if she deemed the entire situation to be mad.

"Lord Willoughby was the gentleman from Vauxhall?" The days that followed their parents' death had been difficult for all of them. Just before news of the tragedy had arrived, however, Tilde had been filled with love sick sighs that had not gone unnoticed. Tilde was surprised that Betsy remembered.

"I was besotted with him at the time, I'll admit, but I'm much older and wiser now. As is he. We've agreed to put our former... inclinations aside. His daughters require a most excellent governess. Not just anyone. They need me. More specifically, Lady Althea needs Peaches and me."

"I remember you––but wait. He kissed you at Lady Elaine's coming out ball? *Last night?*"

Tilde bit her lip. "It was an unfortunate relapse. I've made it quite clear that there shall be no more of that. In fact, it is forgotten."

Betsy threw her hands in the air and burst into a fit of giggles. "You do remember that I was once *engaged?* Do you not? If you two were attracted to one another enough to––how did you put it?" Another fit of giggles. "Relapse? Oh, Tilde. How are you going to fight it while residing in the same household?"

Tilde bent over and buried her face in her hands. "I don't know. But we have to. If you saw those two little girls, you would understand. I could have said no to him, in fact I'm certain Miss Briggs at the agency would have understood. But Lady Eloise, she pretends to be so grown up in order to watch over her sister. She does it for her father too. She worries about her father. I could see it in her eyes. And Lady Althea is afraid to trust. But she trusts Peaches, Betsy, and I believe she will come to trust me. It would have been selfish of me to say no."

Betsy moved across to sit beside Tilde, dropping one arm around her shoulders. "You always were the soft–hearted one of all of us." She squeezed her tight and then rubbed Tilde's arm vigorously. "It's no use worrying over any of this now. What's done is done. And you know I have every faith in you."

Tilde glanced up in time to see a teasing glint in her sister's gaze as she added, "Besides, if anyone can resist future *relapses*, it is my big sister. Furthermore, if you lose your job, you can always come work for me." Which had Tilde groaning and her minx of a sister rolling on the bed laughing.

Because both of them knew that despite getting the highest marks in all of her graduating class at Miss Primm's Ladies' Seminary, Tilde's sewing skills were highly questionable.

* * *

JASPER DID something he'd not done in over four years.

Just as any titled gentlemen would choose to do when feeling the pressures of his duties, he visited one of his clubs. Surprisingly, he was met with a number of familiar faces. It seemed that most of his cohorts from school hadn't really changed all that much. Many had married, set up their nurseries, and then gone on to live their lives the same as they had before.

"Willy!" Archibald Crampton, Viscount Bridgeport, was one of the few who'd avoided the parson's trap. Not for lack of opportunity but because he simply seemed to be having too much of a good time as a bachelor.

Genuine pleasure struck Jasper at the sight of his old school-mate. Bridgeport and he had been polar opposites as youths and even more so as young men. And yet they'd been the best of friends.

Bridge strode across the room and enclosed Jasper in a welcoming embrace, pounding him on the back in greeting. "Good to see you, old man. Come sit down and tell me if you're still following all the rules? How's that working out for you, Willy?" The words were in jest, and yet they stung.

Because to be quite truthful, it hadn't worked out all that well after all.

Except for Althea and Eloise. They would always be the very best part of his life.

Bridge poured two glasses of scotch and slid one across the table. Over the first three slugs, they discussed parliamentary issues, the next three drams were reserved for estate burdens, and after that they both stopped counting.

And of course, eventually, they discussed women.

Bridgeport had nearly married the year before but been jilted at the alter by his bride for a lowly solicitor. Jasper knew that even if Bridge had loved the gel, he'd never show it publicly. Even so… "You holding up? After that business with Lady Caroline?"

His friend shrugged and then grimaced. "My pride suffers more than my heart. Already moving on." He lifted the glass to his lips. "Although I'm not inclined to get myself caught again anytime soon."

"What about you, Wills?" Of course, all of the ton knew of Estelle's untimely passing.

Jasper shrugged. "She hadn't been well for some time." The night had grown quite late by now, inviting an unusual intimacy. Staring into his glass, he swirled the amber liquid and gazed at the reflecting candlelight. "Have you ever been in love, Bridge?"

"Hell, isn't there that one girl in all of our lives? The one we lost? Haunting us in our moments of weakness? Damn shame about Lady Willoughby though… My deepest sympathies. Quite the looker, she was."

Jasper had to concede his deceased wife's beauty. Could she be the treasure he'd lost? She ought to have been. The fact that he'd found himself resenting her over the course of her illness haunted him. If he were being honest with himself, he'd resented her before she even became ill. She'd been so damn set on fulfilling her duty.

He'd watched Estelle push their daughters away, dismiss them when they had gone to her for comfort. At times it seemed she'd bemoaned their very existence.

Treasure he'd lost...

"Who got away from you, Bridge?" Jasper asked. He would not dwell on his own sorry circumstances.

Bridge, a giant of a man with thick black hair and unlikely emerald eyes, leaned back in his chair and chewed on his cheroot. "My cousin's music teacher. Damned beautiful girl. Talented, smart," Wink. "As randy for me as I was for her."

Jasper didn't need to hear any more. The girl hadn't been quality, too far below a viscount to allow for anything more than a fling. He knew how these stories ended. "You loved her?"

A faraway look entered his friends gaze. "And lost her. Wasn't meant to be." And then tipping back the remainder of his glass, he swallowed and then added. "Her hourglass shape will haunt me forever though."

"Was the countess the love of your life? Or did some other lass get away from you?"

Jasper couldn't dishonor Estelle, as much as he wished to unburden himself. But a voice speaking with an indiscernible accent sliced through the fog of his inebriation... *The secret to finding your future lies in the fortune you lost in your past...*

"There was one lady, before Estelle." He spoke into the flickering light. "Felt like I'd found that missing piece of myself. For some reason I didn't realize it at the time. Why are we such fools, Bridge? Why don't we recognize something special when knocked over the head with it?"

He'd meant to visit Miss Fortune the day after that night at the gardens. He'd intended to take her driving in a new curricle he'd purchased a few weeks before. But then he'd failed to follow through... He'd been distracted by his mother's requests. Had he been carrying out his duty or had he been manipulated by tradition?

It didn't matter now.

The fortune from his past never existed. He'd thought himself in love for one evening. One kiss. Both of them were different people now. His daughters came first, and Miss Fortune seemed to be what they needed most. He glanced at his fob watch. He was to meet with her early the following morning.

Perhaps Miss Fortune wasn't as altruistic as he'd believe. Perhaps, knowing she held him over the barrel somewhat with Althea's affection for her dog, she intended to demand an exorbitant salary.

Only he knew this would not be the case. How did he know? He just did. It was as though he'd known the damn woman his entire life.

And yet she remained a mystery.

Setting his glass on the table, Jasper rose reluctantly. She'd be arriving to discuss terms in less than five hours. "It's been a pleasure, Bridge." And it truly had been. He'd kept himself isolated too long.

Not that he didn't come in contact with others while managing Warwick Place, but always those interactions centered around work. And as either landlord or employer to most of them, he treated them with due respect, but could not afford to treat them as friends.

It had been pleasant to spend an evening with a gentleman with whom he was not responsible for in any way, nor the welfare of his family.

Bridge rose to engulf him in another of his giant hugs. "Don't be a stranger, Wills."

Jasper could make no promises.

He'd intended upon spending the entire season in town but had forgotten how difficult his mother could be. And if Miss Fortune were to change her mind about taking the position, he'd have to start all over again.

He refused to hire anyone recommended by his mother.

CHAPTER 10

WELCOME, MISS FORTUNE

*T*he same disapproving butler opened the door for Tilde the following morning at exactly three minutes before eight. And again, he scowled down at Peaches.

"Lord Willoughby is expecting me," Tilde informed him. "Us," she corrected. Best the servants of the house become used to Peaches.

"Right this way."

The austere gentleman led her in a different direction this time, to Willoughby's study she presumed.

But when he opened the door, she was taken aback by the sight before her eyes. Jasper lay sleeping on the settee with Lady Althea on top of him, head tucked beneath his chin. Lady Eloise was sitting at the large desk writing in a small journal.

When Tilde went to step inside, Lady Eloise raised one finger to her lips and whispered. "Thea had nightmares again, so Papa brought us down to his ossiff."

Indeed.

Although he had loosened his cravat, the poor man had fallen asleep wearing his boots. He had tucked one arm under his head as a makeshift pillow but draped his other protectively around

79

his daughter. If Tilde was correct, the garments he wore were the same he'd been wearing yesterday.

As she stepped closer, she could easily make out his full day's growth of beard and dark circles etched beneath his eyes.

Lady Althea, in nightclothes, lay wrapped in a miniature sized quilt. Soft, even snoring sounds, emitted from both father and daughter.

Tiptoeing carefully back across the room, Tilde pulled up the chair near Eloise, placed Peaches on the floor, and then joined the miniature adult at the desk.

"Are you writing letters?" Tilde opened up her pelisse and withdrew a small notebook and pencil.

Which immediately drew Lady Eloise's attention. "What's that?"

"I make it a practice to take note of anything significant when beginning a new post."

"Am I of signific–singivicence?" She leaned forward in an attempt to see the notebook contents better.

"Oh, absolutely. If you're writing letters, then that tells me that you can read and write. That's very important for a teacher to know about her students, wouldn't you agree?"

Lady Eloise nodded. "But I'm not writing letters." She admitted with a frown. "I'm drawing pictures."

"How lovely! I've not much talent for drawing, myself. May I look at yours?"

Lady Eloise hopped off her seat and came around the desk with her sketch book. After biting her bottom lip for a few seconds, she tentatively handed it over.

At the front of the book, the drawings were exactly what Tilde would expect of a five-year-old intelligent little girl. A family. Trees. Fish. Dogs. Tilde smiled. "Is this one Peaches?" The legs were short and the body long.

Eloise nodded.

But as Tilde flipped the pages toward the end of the book, a sick feeling settled into the pit of her stomach. "Who is this?" She pointed at a drawing of a woman with pointed teeth and devilish looking eyes. The woman looked as though she were breathing fire toward a little girl with dark hair.

Eloise stared at the floor. "She's the monster lady who comes in the middle of the night."

Tilde swallowed hard. "Is she a real person?"

But Lady Eloise did not answer, choosing instead to reach out and take back the journal. "I want to learn how to paint, too. Papa's mama says we're too young to learn to paint but Papa said he'd see what he could do. Are you going to teach us to paint, Miss Fortune?"

Tilde, still shaken from the unusual drawing, and from Lady Eloise's explanation, forced herself to focus on the question at hand. And in that moment, she had no doubt that she'd do whatever was necessary to bring some comfort and security to these children's lives.

"You see," Tilde retrieved her own notebook and pencil from the desk. "This is exactly the sort of significant information I must take note of." And then she read aloud what she was writing, "Lady Eloise wishes to learn to paint. Task. Purchase necessary supplies."

When she glanced back up, a pleased smile danced on Eloise's lips.

"Do you have bad dreams too?" She could not help but wonder, realizing that the child had similar dark circles to her father's beneath her smaller, but equally expressive, gray eyes.

Eloise began to answer but then her gaze flicked behind Tilde at rustling sounds from across the room. Jasper was doing his best to arrange Lady Althea on the settee without waking her.

"What in the world?" Jasper had sat up and was staring at Tilde with confused eyes.

Tilde glanced meaningfully at the clock. "Our appointment, my lord."

She could see the moment he realized what he'd done. Pitiful man that he was.

He scrubbed one hand down his face and groaned. "I must beg your forgiveness for, what now? The fifth time? And if I'm correct, you've yet to grant it for my last two transgressions."

"Lady Eloise has kept me well occupied." Tilde sat up straight. He seemed at a loss, so she decided to take matters into her own hands. "If you'll remember, it was I who requested this meeting. So, might I make a suggestion?"

He blinked his eyes at her and then nodded slowly, reminding her how Eloise had done the same a few minutes before. "Seeing as it was you, indeed, who suggested the meeting… By all means."

Tilde rose. "If Lady Eloise and you would be so kind as to show me and Peaches to the nursery, I will assist them in their morning routine, and when you have completed your ablutions, you may send for me for our interview."

Lady Eloise stepped forward, holding Peaches' leading string in one hand and her drawing book in the other. "You carry Thea, Papa, and I shall be the leader."

"Excellent idea," Tilde commended her for her efficient manner of thinking.

"Interview?" Jasper raised his brows. "Did we not dispense with such a need yesterday?"

"On your part, indeed, I believe we did." She followed Lady Eloise to the large wooden door and then glanced over her shoulder to ascertain that he followed. "It is I who shall be interviewing you."

JASPER EASED himself into the hot bath Cummings had ordered and groaned. Not only did his head feel as though a horse stepped on it last night, but his stomach heaved at the notion of eating any breakfast. And apparently now he was to be interrogated by his daughters' new governess.

The temptation to laugh warred with a temptation to send her packing.

He dismissed both and groaned again instead.

"Another nightmare, my lord?" Cummings asked before pouring some heated water over his head.

"Eloise was sitting up with her when I came up to check on them after I got home."

Cummings tsked. "You know I never involve myself in your personal affairs, my lord, but I don't like that Crabtree woman the Countess has put in charge of them. She has a cruel look to her."

Jasper had thought much the same and ignored the worry as being overprotective. Had he wrongly assumed his own mother would not have the girls' best interest at heart? He could only be grateful that Tilde was here now.

Miss Fortune.

"Their new governess begins today. I cannot say I am not happy for that."

"Very good, my lord." Cummings set the soap in Jasper's hand and then busied himself across the room.

But Jasper wondered something. "Have you ever witnessed Mrs. Crabtree treat the girls inappropriately?"

Cummings brushed at the waistcoat hanging on the dressing room door and sighed. "That's a difficult question. There are some folks who quite literally believe the biblical directive that by not sparing the rod, they risked spoiling the child. Some who use it as an excuse even... "

Jasper's heart sank to the pit of his stomach. It would not happen under his own roof. He'd made himself clear to Mrs. Crabtree that she was already on thin ice with him. It made no difference that the woman had been in his mother's employ for nigh two decades.

Lord Willoughby slid down so as to submerge himself completely in the large tub and did not come up until he could hold his breath no longer.

Thank God Miss Fortune had arrived.

FORTY MINUTES LATER, feeling more himself and less like something the butler had dragged in from the front step, Jasper sat at his desk awaiting his daughters' new governess. His heart should not feel lighter as he anticipated her arrival, nor should he find it necessary to smother a rogue fantasy based on how she'd felt in his arms less than forty-eight hours before.

He cleared his throat. Theirs would be a professional relationship from this point forward.

Three short raps signaled her arrival. He had no need to ask who it might be. She was the only one who would knock as though the inhabitant would bid her enter immediately.

"Who is it?" He smiled to himself.

Eyes that appeared more green than brown today peered around the door. Without permission, the rest of her followed. "Did you not send for me?" A frown puckered her forehead.

More alert now, his eyes roved over the drab gray garment she'd been wearing earlier. It was now partially covered by a crisp white apron. With her hair pinned into a low knot at the back of her head, she appeared every inch the strait-laced governess.

A governess of whom his baser instincts urged him to muss up. He'd managed to repair her chignon once; he could do it again.

And then he immediately pushed such inappropriate thoughts from his mind.

"Lord Willoughby." Her voice already sounded like a reprimand, as though she were reading his mind. Looking adorably studious and serious minded, she opened her notebook and removed a pencil from behind her ear. "I trust you're feeling more yourself now."

He nodded, wondering what she'd already written in her tidy little notebook. His pounding head had subsided, and Cummings had assured him that his complexion no longer tinged green.

"Much. And the girls? Have they given you any trouble this morning?"

She scowled. Had he insulted her? "If they had, then I most certainly would not be the governess I expect of myself."

"Very well…" He began to laugh but then caught himself at her offended expression. And then belatedly, he rose. "Won't you sit down?" He gestured to the chair across from him.

"Thank you. I will." Despite all of her bravado, he noticed she avoided his gaze. Which, he admitted to himself, was for the best. They'd made a pact.

The girls needed her.

Miss Fortune tucked a stray hair behind her ear and then cleared her throat. "I always interview the parents of my charges before writing any lesson plans. It's in everyone's best interests to establish a greater understanding of one another's expectations."

In her element now, she finally met his gaze; unsmiling. So stern and yet she'd already exhibited an abundance of compassion toward his children.

Again, he knew she was the perfect governess for Althea and Eloise. "Sound thinking Miss Fortune."

She narrowed her eyes at him, and he stared back somberly. After a few interesting moments, in which she had apparently become convinced of his sincerity, she returned her gaze to that notebook of hers and fired off her first question.

"Do your daughters have a favorite toy, and what is it?" She awaited his answer, pencil poised. "These questions may seem frivolous to you," she explained, "but your answers provide me with vital information."

About him... It seemed Miss Fortune had a few tricks up her sleeve. He quite approved.

How was it that being grilled by her did not annoy him? She was a governess, for God's sake!

Contrarily, he found her quite entertaining.

"Eloise has a doll she loves, named Breanne. Althea has a stuffed dog... Eloise tells me the dog has recently been renamed..."

"Peaches." They spoke together in unison. Green and brown today, he noticed. And hints of blue. Her eyes fascinated him.

Miss Fortune blinked hard and glanced down at her notes again. "In your opinion, can you tell me what Lady Eloise is passionate about?"

Ah, this question was trickier. "In the practical sense, I'd say, her sister. Purely for enjoyment, she loves to draw. And Althea, I wish I knew. She loves flowers though and always wants to pick them for our housekeeper at Warwick Place. She also enjoys assisting Cook with baking. But she doesn't tell me any of this."

But Miss Fortune was smiling. Not a dazzling or flirtatious smile, rather a satisfied one. "Not all children are vocal about their interests. What's important is that you have watched them. You would be surprised..." She pinched those lips of hers together and glanced back down at her notebook.

"What are your girls afraid of?"

He swallowed hard at this one. At times he thought he knew, but he'd been unable to offer the reassurances they seemed to need. "I believe they're frightened of me leaving them," he admitted.

Tilde nodded solemnly, writing something down, and then without skipping a beat moved on to the next question.

"What are the nightmares about?"

Jasper bristled at this one. He'd asked Thea every time and she had never given him an answer.

"It kills me. Her shyness." He clenched his fists. "And it started before Estelle, before my wife, passed on. And as much as I appreciate that Eloise can relay her sister's words to me, at times I wonder if she's crippling her."

"I've seen such a phenomenon between twins before, although not quite to this extent. But they are young, Jasper. You'd be surprised how resilient children can be."

Her use of his name warmed him like a crackling fire at Christmastime.

"She's watching over Peaches for me right now. Talking up a storm. Showing my dog where all of her toys are and making sure Peaches knows the rules of the house."

This woman could not know how much of a relief her words brought him. He exhaled loudly.

"Inform me immediately if anyone gives you any trouble at all. Mrs. Crabtree, my mother––anyone. Or if you have need of any particular supplies."

And for the first time, in her capacity as his employee, she seemed uncertain of herself. She reached into her pocket and removed a piece of paper. When she held it out to him, that same sinking feeling he'd had with Cummings' comment hit him.

Drawn by a child's hand, a terrifying woman stood over a dark–haired little girl breathing fire.

"There are others like this, by both of the girls. They both draw. This one is Eloise's," she extracted another. "And Althea drew this one for me. Eloise says the lady in the picture is the monster lady."

"I wondered if she is the woman of Althea's nightmares. Perhaps she's told Eloise about them?"

But Jasper was seeing red. It had to be Mrs. Crabtree. He'd warned the woman not to punish his children. He jerked his head. "You will keep me informed?"

The red was disappearing and the blood in his veins turned ice cold.

Miss Fortune reached out to take the drawings back, but he shook his head. "Leave them."

He was vaguely aware that she closed her book and replaced the pencil behind her ear before standing up.

He'd not protected his daughters. Now they had nightmares and drew pictures of a woman who never should have been left alone with them. Mrs. Crabtree was finished.

"Miss Fortune?" He forced the words from his mouth. "Tilde?"

She'd been making her way toward the door, but his voice halted her.

"Yes?"

"Thank you."

Her chin dipped and without looking back, she answered. "You're welcome, Jasper."

CHAPTER 11

HIS MOTHER

*T*ilde held the door wide for Peaches to precede her from the nursery into her own chamber and then closed it quietly behind them so as not to awaken the twins.

Nap time was always a welcome respite. Not that the girls were difficult, but it gave her time to plan the next day's lessons and take care of any personal business. Today, she'd write a letter to her former pupils, sew a new button on one of her gowns, and give Peaches some well needed attention.

All the while doing her best to avoid drumming up errant thoughts about her increasingly handsome employer, who she rarely saw but made numerous appearances in her dreams.

Although Jasper had made it a point to pop into the nursery each morning, Parliament was in full swing and he often didn't return until late in the evenings. He made the most of his time spent with his girls, however, providing them with his full attention.

While writing in her lesson book on the occasion of one of his morning visits, Tilde had overheard him explaining to the twins that since he'd been voting by proxy over the past few years, he had lots of learning to do. When he'd gone on to explain what proxy meant, Tilde had given up all pretense of her task at hand in order to watch daughters and father interact.

His love for them was obvious, as was all the frustration of being their sole parent. He'd proven on more than one occasion, already, that he wanted to do what was best for his children, but unfortunately, his mother seemed to thwart his efforts at every turn.

Much as she attempted to do with Tilde.

While Jasper was away, his mother dropped all pretense of caring for the well-being of her granddaughters and only took notice of them when an opportunity arose to parade them in front of her afternoon guests––much as she would a favorite toy or pet. She'd insist the girls be dressed and styled immaculately, and always identically, and then have them make their curtseys to her visitors so they could exclaim at the girls' likeness to one another and try to guess which one was which.

Althea struggled increasingly in her abilities to finish her studies after such meetings and it seemed the girl took one step forward and then fell two steps back.

If only Jasper was not gone so very often, because despite Tilde's bravado on occasion, Jasper's mother, for all her evil ways, was the Lady of the house, a countess, a peer. And Tilde only the governess. If Tilde were to lose her position it was not she who would suffer, but Althea and Eloise.

The situation was becoming most untenable. She was going to have to find an opportunity to speak with Jasper about the problem. Although he'd insisted upon hiring her when his mother disapproved, in many things, the befuddled man failed to comprehend the countess' manipulations.

Lady Willoughby was wily in her subtle ways, indeed. But she could not hide her true nature all of the time.

Tilde trusted her about as far as she could throw her.

Unfortunately, the problem was not an uncomplicated one.

With a sigh, Tilde untied her apron and laid it across her bed next to where she'd placed Peaches.

When she'd first arrived, her chamber had housed three small twin beds, three matching short dressers and one austere desk and chair. She was surprised, however, when after taking the girls and Peaches for a walk through the park on her second afternoon there, she returned to find that the furnishings had been completely overhauled. Although adjacent to the nursery, the new canopied bed, desk, vanity and wardrobe seemed more suited for that of an esteemed guest than even the most prominent servant in the household.

Jasper had asked her that evening if she found the new furnishings to her liking and when she'd gone to thank him, he'd cut her off with a satisfied nod. She had the feeling he'd ordered the improvements himself. Lady Willoughby certainly would not have.

It had been a kind gesture, indeed.

She glanced at the watch attached to her chatelaine. The girls had gone down for their nap a short while ago, and most likely wouldn't awaken for another hour. Atop Tilde's luxurious bed, Peaches had located one of the pillows, walked around in several tight rings and then settled into a comfortable circle of dog. Tilting her head to the left, she watched Tilde with mild curiosity.

"You think you deserve a nap yourself, do you?" Tilde raised one eyebrow at her dog.

Peaches tilted her head to the right.

"Yes, well. I could not be happier with your behavior this week." Tilde rubbed Peaches' back and dropped a kiss on the top of her tiny head.

Even Mr. Yardley, the butler who'd been so skeptical upon her initial arrival, was warming to the idea of having a dog in the house. Many servants, however had not.

Furthermore, Tilde doubted Lady Willoughby or Mrs. Crabtree, who'd gone back to acting as the countess' assistant, would ever hold any affection for Peaches. Staring at her dog, she frowned. Not everyone had the good sense to appreciate the presence of a well–behaved canine companion.

And some human beings were simply cold-hearted at best.

Since showing Jasper those drawings, Tilde was relieved that Mrs. Crabtree had been blessedly absent from the nursery. And if Tilde was not mistaken, Eloise seemed slightly less guarded. Althea spoke often to Peaches, but still hadn't addressed Tilde directly.

Peaches perked up, ears alert, and then a knock sounded on the door. It would not be Lord Willoughby; she rebuked her racing heart. He'd departed for the Palace of Westminster early this morning and would likely not return until after sundown. And, but of course, he would not come to her bed chamber. That would be the height of impropriety. He would send a servant if he needed to speak with her.

Opening the door, Tilde did her best to hide her dismay.

Lady Willoughby stood tapping her foot on the carpeted floor in the corridor, albeit, a friendly smile stretching her lips. "May I come in?"

Tilde gestured for the woman to enter. She was as suspicious of this unlikely visit as Peaches appeared to be. "What can I do for you, my lady." Tilde hoped this visit did not portend another performance by the twins.

She would most definitely speak with Jasper about them this evening. Even if it required that she wait up until midnight.

The woman strolled around the room inquisitively, examining one of the ornately carved bedposts, and then glancing in the mirror above the elegant vanity. "My son has excellent taste. Would you not agree?"

Tilde merely nodded, both oddly pleased and uncomfortable to know that Jasper –– *her employer* –– had chosen the lavish furnishings himself –– for her bedchamber, no less.

"I must admit," Lady Willoughby began, "I had misgivings when you first arrived."

Tilde's back stiffened instinctively. "I cannot imagine why. My references are impeccable."

Lady Willoughby chuckled and slid a knowing glance in Tilde's direction. "I am not unaware of your past acquaintance with my son."

Good Heavens!

"My son keeps nothing from me, and the decision to hire you was one we discussed at great length. In the end, Lady Althea's well-being was what mattered most."

The woman's words failed to ring true. But how else would Lady Willoughby have known what occurred all those years ago? "In that case, my lady," Tilde would make the most of this sudden altruism for Lady Althea. "Parading the girls before your guests at a moment's notice has had a most detrimental effect on both of them. Not only does it interrupt their schedule, taking them away from their lessons, but the stress from these… visits… robs them of their ability to pay attention afterward."

Lady Willoughby pursed her lips, and appeared as though she was going to argue, but then pivoted and strode across the room to stare out the window.

Tilde met Peaches' curious gaze. Her pup tilted her head questioningly and Tilde shrugged with a frown.

"Be that as it may," the older woman turned back to face Tilde. A cold emptiness lurked in the back of her eyes. "Your ability to provide adequate supervision for the twins has provided a sense of relief for Lord Willoughby. With such concerns resolved, you and the children will likely be travelling to Warwick Place within the next fortnight. It's important that my son be able to direct all of his attentions on Lady Elaine before they make their announcement."

Tilde caught her breath. Of course, Lady Althea and Eloise spoke fondly of their father's country estate and the servants there, but they had a close relationship with their papa. It was significantly plausible to believe the girls might suffer upon him absenting himself from their precarious little lives. He'd told her himself that he thought their greatest fear was separation from him.

Tilde wondered that he'd not be more concerned for their well-being.

Most children of aristocratic families spent inordinate amounts of time separated from their parents, but Tilde had believed Lord Willoughby to view his relationship with his daughters differently.

And that was the only reason Tilde felt an unreasonable urge to cry. Not because the thought of him marrying the duke's beautiful daughter crushed her heart.

Because it didn't.

It. Did. Not.

Tilde nodded. She'd travelled often enough with her other charges and never given it a second thought. Why, then, did the notion of taking these girls far away from their father leave her feeling unsettled?

It had nothing to do with the fact that Tilde, too, would be leaving him.

Nothing. At. All.

She nodded. "I'm sure Lord Willoughby will wish to do whatever is best for his daughters."

"Which first and foremost is to ensure his succession." Lady Willoughby's voice could have cut through ice. "You'll be informed as soon as the arrangements have been finalized."

And then, as quickly as she'd arrived, the disconcerting woman departed.

Tilde paced across to the bed, lifted Peaches into her arms and cradled her beneath her chin.

Lord Willoughby—Jasper—had hired Tilde, and yet he'd been noticeably absent these past few days. Was he feeling the pressure of his position in the House of Lords? Or was he merely keeping himself away from her so that neither of them was tempted by their previous inclinations?

Inclinations which had been quite successful at keeping Tilde awake at night.

On more than one occasion, she'd caught him watching her from those dark and smoky eyes of his. And she'd done her best not to gaze back hungrily. The children were their priority.

She might have had an easier time of it, if she'd not come to see that his character was proving to be more handsome than even his exterior.

They could not go on like this, surely? Perhaps that was why he'd chosen to send her and the children away.

Or perhaps she was wrong about all of it. Perhaps she'd only imagined that his looks held passion and longing.

Conceivably, he regretted the liberties they'd taken with one another at the Duchess of Marvelle's ball. She'd been in his employ for over a fortnight now and he'd managed quite well to avoid her. Perhaps his mother was not a villain at all… She was merely the messenger. If so, then his meaning was loud and clear. Tilde meant nothing more to him than any other person in his employ.

Shuffling sounds drifted over from the girls' room next door, forcing Tilde to put the matter from her mind.

She'd promised them a walk in the park with Peaches. It was exactly what Tilde needed as well. The tension in this house could be too much to stand at times. She set Peaches on the floor and together they went through the adjoining door to assist the girls in preparing to go out.

Only a few clouds hovered in the sky, but even if rain fell down in droves, Tilde would have insisted on this outing.

The urge for fresh air seemed more pressing than ever.

* * *

95

JASPER TIPPED his hat to one of his mother's friends as she passed him on the sidewalk. He'd sent John Coachman ahead, preferring to walk this afternoon. Session had adjourned early and for the first time in days he found some time to himself.

On impulse, he crossed the road and entered the Park. It was early and so all of society had yet to have descended upon the popular venue in which one went to see and be seen.

He ought to have ridden home in the coach so that he could spend the afternoon tackling the reports he'd received from the estate manager at Warwick Place. Also awaiting him was the new bill Lord Fitzhume had asked him to support.

And yet.

He kicked a stone that appeared in the path at his feet.

Having Miss Fortune for the girls' governess was turning into a special form of torture for him. Without fail, she sat at her desk working vigilantly when he visited the nursery, seemingly intent upon sabotaging all of his efforts to ignore her.

Brushing her hair from her cheek.

Sighing breathily.

Licking her lips.

Touching the edge of her bodice, drawing his attention to…

Throughout all of it, Jasper had done his best to not allow his gaze to linger on her for too long.

Fighting whatever this was between them was proving to be exhausting. She haunted his dreams incessantly, and it was even worse when he lay in bed awake. Knowing she slept under the same roof, imagining her in nothing but a night rail, and then less. The temptation to go to her left him clutching himself beneath the sheets like a randy youth.

He'd caught up with the stone he kicked, retrieved it with his hand, and sent it flying up into the treetops.

If he returned to his house that very moment, he'd do some-thing inappropriate. God help him.

At the same time, Eloise was smiling more, and Althea was

more animated than he could ever remember seeing her. He could not jeopardize losing her services.

He'd been walking through a copse of trees and thought himself quite all alone. But then he heard the laughter of children's voices. And a sharp excited barking sound, and then, "Peaches. Come back here this instant!"

Miss Fortune.

Everything rational in his brain urged him to turn around and make for home. He could spend his afternoon being productive without the distraction of knowing her to be under the same roof.

And yet his legs strode purposely in the direction of the blanket spread out upon the grass.

"Papa!" Eloise caught sight of him and was holding a cluster of flowers in the air. "Look, we've made crowns out of dandelions! Have you come to join us for tea? Look Miss Fortune, Papa's come to join us."

Jasper's breath caught in his throat when his *daughters' governess* turned to look at him. How had he ever thought that she was not beautiful? He'd been wrong. Utterly so.

With a wreath of flowers propped upon her head, her eyes danced with laughter and her smile came easily. He caught her gaze with his own, and held it, lost in the depths of greens and browns.

Until something flickered behind there, and she glanced downward. When she lifted her chin again, she scowled in disapproval. "Good afternoon, Lord Willoughby. If you've come to fetch the girls for another of your mother's at homes, then I must object. Your daughters are twins, yes, but little girls were not created so that they could be paraded in front of a bunch of windbags and gossips for an afternoon's entertainment."

Althea had come running up to him, along with the dog on a leading string. She wound her frail looking arms around his leg and made a seat of his foot.

"Hello, sweetheart." He patted the top of her head. Confused at Miss Fortune's accusations, he limped cautiously toward the scowling lady.

"Good afternoon to you as well, Miss Fortune." And then he bowed. To his governess. "And what are you going on about? My mother is doing what?"

"Your mother––" She began. But with a meaningful glance at the girls, clamped her lips shut. "This is difficult."

Jasper could not disagree with her. "I realize––"

"But that's the problem, Jasper." She took a deep breath. "Lady Brightly, my former employer. She had an older sister who visited often. The sister was rather… religious minded, and on several occasions attempted to have a say in how I did my job. And I am always open to constructive criticism. Don't get me wrong. But this woman. She came to me stating that I was too lenient. That my lesson plans ought to be centered upon scripture, and prayer and less on math and history. I was filling the girl's heads, she insisted, with thoughts they'd never need, confusing them with heathen philosophies and blasphemous science. The first time this happened, I had only been with the family for a little over a year and, truth be told… I doubted myself."

That surprised him. But then he remembered the naïve girl he'd met years ago and could imagine her younger self feeling hesitant about her convictions. "But you spoke with Lady Brightly. Did you not? After all, they were her children."

Tilde met his eyes. "I did Jasper. And in truth, I had been a little zealous with my teachings. But we worked together to incorporate aspects of their faith into some of the lessons. And I realized all the teachings could be richer for it."

"I don't understand."

"Lady Brightly was *there*. She was the lady of the house as well as my employer. It was not my responsibility to deal with her overly righteous sister on my own. And Jasper, most important of all: she saw her sister for who she was."

"You can come to me any time--" But Tilde was shaking her head.

"You do not see your mother. You must open your eyes, and your ears, and understand with your heart, who your mother is." And then she dropped her gaze to the ground. "And what she is doing to your most precious treasures."

In that moment, a glimmer of understanding taunted his conscience but at the same time pierced his very identity. "She is manipulative, Tilde, I realize this, but that's only because..." But Tilde was shaking her head.

"Step back for a moment, but watch her closely, Jasper."

Her words rang true, for the most part.

And then he nodded. "I will speak with her."

Jasper stared across the blanket to wear his daughters were carefully tying dandelions into a chain. His mother was all too aware of Althea's shyness around other people, or she should be, anyhow. But only last week he'd had to squash her inclination to punish his daughter for it. He closed his eyes, hoping Matilda was wrong. The very notion that his mother would require the girls to leave their school room in order for her guests to gape and stare... "I will speak with her," he spoke again, this time through gritted teeth. "You have my word."

He lowered himself to the grass and Althea promptly crawled across the blanket and settled onto his lap, Peaches followed and cuddled into his daughter's much smaller one.

Jasper's promise seemed to subdue Miss Fortune's irritation and yet... something still seemed to be bothering her.

"Thea," Eloise hopped up and down. "The ducks are swimming close. Miss Fortune, may we feed them the bread crumbs now?"

All attention again focused on her charges, Miss Fortune opened the basket and handed Althea a familiar looking bag. "But

I'll have to hold the leading string for now, darling," she explained. "Or Peaches will chase all the ducks away."

Jasper's gaze followed his two daughters as they skipped to the water's edge and began gently tossing treats to the fowl. "They can be a handful, I'll admit, but…" He shook his head. How could he explain the love he felt for those two little urchins?

"They're rather like having a handful of wonder, or rainbows, or laughter." She chuckled. And he knew exactly what she meant.

He turned and met her eyes. "So, you have no additional scolds for me?" A smile tugged at his lips. Why did the idea of her scolding him raise his temperature ever so slightly?

She leaned back. The dog settled onto the blanket. Jasper realized her hand was only a scant few inches away from his.

"Is it true you plan on sending the girls back to Warwick Place soon?" A trace of disappointment lingered in her question.

As matter of fact, he had considered sending them back with their new governess…

Initially.

The idea had seemed so rational at the time. And when he'd mentioned it to his mother she'd readily agreed.

"I had considered it." He admitted. "I had doubts as to how they'd fare in the city. I knew Parliament would demand a good deal of my time and…" He'd planned on finding a lady to marry. But now that he'd arrived, and met Lady Elaine and a few of the other, oh, so very young debutantes, he had no desire to send his daughters away from him.

He had no desire to send Miss Fortune away.

Despite numerous sleepless nights and frustrating days.

The air between them hung thick and heavy. He vibrated inside. Staring down at their hands, he edged his one inch closer to hers.

"I," she began and then cleared her throat. "I believe they would miss you a great deal." Had her hand moved a fraction of an inch closer to his?

Eloise squealed, distracting him a moment. Several of the ducks fled back into the water and Althea threw a handful of bread at them. Eloise took Althea's hand and the girls jumped up and down. "Come back, ducks! Come back!"

Miss Fortune's laughter echoed his own in a moment of pure contentment. He moved his hand closer, so that his pinky finger barely skimmed hers.

She did not attempt to draw it away.

"I would miss them." He admitted gruffly. And then he added, "I would miss you."

A connective energy seemed to spark where their fingers met, almost as though a current flowed between them. All his senses homed in on the warmth of her skin, her slightest motion, the way her breath hitched when he traced his finger along the length of hers.

And yet they barely touched.

The tumult of satisfaction coursing through him was some-what terrifying. Because along with satisfaction flowed need. And he knew, by God, that touching her hand would never be enough.

He glanced sideways in time to see her swallow hard and then bite her lip. Indeed, they'd promised not to act upon any incli-nations.

She blinked a few times and then -- "Mrs. Crabtree has stayed away. I haven't found any new drawings."

Swallowing hard, he then cleared his throat. She was right, of course.

"I thank you for bringing the situation to my attention." Jasper despised himself for not ridding the nursery of that woman earlier. Since then, the circles beneath Eloise's eyes had lightened. She'd not awakened him to come to the nursery since Tilde's first disastrous morning.

"Perhaps the nightmares will not return."

They both sat in silence, the touch of their hands hardly more than a whisper. Sitting on the grass with her on a warm spring afternoon, he would not even attempt to deny, not only the desire, but the belonging he felt in that moment.

He'd kissed her over a decade ago––and had remembered the night with more than a little fondness. More recently, he'd held her and kissed her in the Duke and Duchess of Marvelle's garden. Ever since, he'd thought of nothing but making her his in every way. She'd become his mecca, his home.

Jasper blinked at his ridiculous metaphors.

He understood his lust for her all too clearly. The other emotions she aroused, however, left him muddled and confused.

"I will not make any plans regarding the girls without discussing them first with you. You needn't worry." He'd reassure her whenever possible. He could not think of her as a woman, and neither could he treat her as an employee.

But now more than ever, he couldn't risk the girls well–being.

"And I shall take your advice regarding my mother into consideration."

She nodded.

And then the girls were running across the grass and the dog jumped up to greet them.

"Now may we partake of our tea, Miss Fortune?" Eloise smoothed her pale blue dress. "Althea is simply starving after all this exercise."

"Do you want to eat, Peaches?" Althea's voice was music to Jasper's ears as she addressed Miss Fortune's dog. It was a little higher sounding than Eloise's. He'd heard it so rarely…

"Won't you join us, my lord?" Miss Fortune was already opening the basket and handing each of the girls a napkin. Jasper took the one she handed him and crawled onto all fours so that he could assist her.

"What have we here? Crumpets and tea?"

"Biscuits and lemonade." A smiled danced on Miss Fortune's lips as she withdrew a handful of small glasses. "And fruit.

Nothing fancy, I'm afraid." And then she handed him the tin of cookies to divvy up amongst their party.

"You know what, Papa?" Eloise nibbled on her cookie. "I don't think ducks like little girls."

"It's not the little girls that they swim away from, sweetheart. It is loud, very high-pitched noises that cause them to retreat."

"Like when I screamed?"

Miss Fortune met his smile with one of her own.

"Like when you scream," he agreed.

CHAPTER 12

*T*ilde sat up at the scream from the room next door. Was it Eloise or Althea?

She fumbled her way through the dark to the adjoining door. She'd so hoped the nightmares had gone away completely.

Moonlight shining through the window slanted across the bed where Althea had curled into a tiny ball and was crying uncontrollably. The sight was enough to draw tears to Tilde's own eyes, but she stifled them. The situation required calm assurances and empathy. Her own loss of composure would hardly diffuse Althea's fears.

Tilde maneuvered herself over to the girl's side, but as she wrapped her arms around Althea, she heard a sniffle from across the room. Eloise was watching from the other bed with her tiny arms hugging her knees to her chest.

"All is well, little Thea. Wake up love. It isn't real. Can you wake up for me, love?" Perspiration drenched Althea's tiny body, and she trembled uncontrollably. Tilde rocked her back and forth.

So intent was Tilde on the child that she hadn't realized the door opened until flickering candlelight caught her eye.

"When did it start?" Jasper's voice managed to relieve some of Tilde's own concern.

She had been caring for children for what felt like most of her life, and yet relief swept through her at the knowledge that she was not to cope with such troubling emotions alone.

"Not long ago. I came as soon as it began."

After setting the candle on one of the bedside tables, he dropped onto the other side of the bed and stroked his daughter's hair. "I'm here, little one. And so is Miss Fortune. You've nothing to be afraid of, you know?"

"Peaches." Althea mumbled into Tilde's nightgown.

"Was the monster lady screaming at Peaches?" Even in the dimly lit room, Tilde could see that Eloise's eyes resembled large saucers.

Althea nodded, her face still tucked beneath Tilde's chin.

The girls' exchange sent shivers racing down Tilde's spine. "Go to your Papa, sweetie and I'll be right back."

Jasper reached forward, and while gathering Althea into his arms, brushed his hands along Tilde's front, grazing her breasts. She shivered at his touch, innocent though it was, and then chastised herself for her response. A child was feeling distressed. A child that was in *her* care.

Ashamed, she lurched off the bed and rushed through the connecting door into her own chamber. Going directly to her bed, she pulled the coverlet down and felt around for Peaches, who, likely having heard the distress coming from the room next door, was already awake.

"Thea needs you, baby." Tilde said, scooping her pup into her arms.

As soon as Peaches hopped into Althea's lap, the little girl's trembling eased.

"See, Peaches is just fine. I'd never let anyone hurt my favorite puppy in the whole world, nor," Tilde glanced from Eloise to Althea. "Either of my favorite little girls."

And easy as that, Althea climbed back under the covers, Peaches crawling in beside her.

"Can Peaches sleep with Thea?" Eloise asked the question for her sister.

Tilde met Jaspers gaze from across the bed and shrugged. "It's fine by me, as long as you don't object."

Jasper ran one hand through his hair and sighed. The two very good friends snuggled peacefully where only moments before had been terror. "How could I object to so much love?"

Tilde smiled and then moved to go back to her own chamber when a tiny hand clasped her wrist. Large eyes stared up at her. Tilde needed no words in order to know the question behind them.

"Thea wants you and Papa to stay until she falls asleep." Eloise had climbed back under her own blanket but was still communicating for her sister.

Jasper leaned against the headboard, lifted his feet onto the bed and crossed them at the ankles. He'd obviously been through this routine before. "I'll stay, Thea. No need for Miss Fortune to miss out on her sleep as well."

But he sounded… lonely.

Tilde made herself comfortable on the chair beside the bed, going so far as to tuck her feet beneath her. Jasper's questioning eyes reminded her a little of his daughter's own silent plea.

"I'll stay a while too." And in the flickering light of the candle, their gazes locked and held.

Was it possible to see into another person's soul? To know not only their thoughts, but to feel what they feel, what they need? She'd never felt so… connected to another person. It made no sense, and yet it was the most natural thing she'd ever experienced.

And when she was with him, she felt every breath of air go into her lungs and fill her body with life. Every touch reminded her she was a part of something much larger than herself. The world was a richer place, and her very reason for being suddenly had meaning.

Staring down at Thea, she marveled at the intimacy of such a night.

"It's nice to not be alone in this." His words startled her from her thoughts. His wife must have sat with him before she became ill; leaving him solely responsible for his daughter's well-being, leaving him with no one to share his concerns, his fears.

Only on this night, he had her.

"I cannot imagine the heartbreak you've experienced." He didn't respond but stared across at her again and then dropped his gaze to his daughter's tousled head. His girls were so very beautiful and yet so very fragile.

"Thank you," he finally whispered.

Tilde glanced up from Althea, whose breathing was now even and deep, and met his gaze. Those silken strands that had wound around her eleven years ago had thickened into ropes. And as the ropes tightened, she struggled to hold anything back from him.

Was it possible that she loved him?

She leaned her head back and closed her eyes. *I cannot love him!* It was impossible. Focus on the children––Tomorrow's lesson plan –– anything but the sensation that her heart was betraying her in the worst possible way…

I cannot love him!

TILDE WOKE with a start as she was lifted into the air. "What are you…"

"Hush." Jasper carried her out of the nursery and through the door to her own chamber. "Both girls have been sleeping for a while. Thea won't relinquish your pup, however."

Tilde could not remember the last time another person had

deigned to carry her. Uncertainty had her clutching her arms around his neck in surprise. "You don't have to…"

He only held her tighter as he turned and managed to close the door behind them.

"Oh, Jasper." Did he not know what his nearness did to her? But by now he was already lowering her onto the high bed he'd selected for her suite.

She expected him to bid her goodnight or thank her. She expected anything but for him to remain standing by the bed, watching her in the moonlight with a dark intensity.

"My heartbreak." He began before looking to stare toward the window. "Was for what should have been. I was not heartbroken when she died. I was… relieved." The words surprised her.

When he turned to gaze down at her again, he seemed to be waiting for her to rebuke him.

Tilde sat up so she could see him better. "Did you not love her?"

He shook his head, almost imperceptibly. "I loved her. She was my wife. I was never *in love* with her. And in the end, I found myself resenting her." The darkness seemed to invite his confidences. She doubted he'd ever admitted so much to anyone else.

"You resented her for being ill?"

"I resented her for disparaging herself. First for not getting with child quickly enough, as though it was something she had any control over. And then for delivering girls instead of an heir. As time wore on, it became her obsession. Even after she became ill…"

Some understanding dawned in Tilde at this information. "She did not love Althea and Eloise? Her own daughters?"

Jasper shook his head sadly. "Perhaps she loved them, but… She never showed it if she did." And in that moment, she saw his pain. Not for himself, but for his daughters who'd needed their mother. For all the disillusionment he'd experienced in his marriage. A pain he hid from the world.

Yes, he was a lord, one of London's most elite. But he was also just a man. One who had refused to allow his daughters to feel neglected. He worried over their upbringing, forfeited the libertine life many of his ilk took for granted, and tormented himself over his daughters' fears.

Tilde leaned forward and then knelt on the edge of the mattress. When she reached out for him, he did not hesitate to walk into her embrace. And then she was in his arms, and he in hers.

"Tilde." His voice broke as his lips claimed hers.

The first kiss had been magical. Their second one had been devastating.

This kiss?

It unleashed the passion that had been denied for far too long. It was raw, desperate. Some rational part of her brain panicked. He was her employer! An earl! This could only lead to disaster. But her body refused to listen. Her need for him took over.

Without breaking the kiss, Jasper crawled onto the bed and hovered over her. And then his body lowered so that she could feel the strength of his thighs, the hardness of his chest, and the intensity of his arousal.

She exulted in his weight as it pressed her into the soft mattress and welcomed the warmth of his body entangled with hers.

A few mere wisps of fabric prevented skin from touching skin. He wore only a dressing gown and night shirt. And she wore only her night rail. His hands had managed to slide beneath it to trail along her leg.

Tilde had long ago determined she'd remain a spinster. She'd given up on the notion of experiencing physical love. She'd convinced herself that it wasn't something she needed in order to have a fulfilling existence.

But as he touched her, she came alive in a way she'd never imagined.

Hunger.

Her body hungered for…

Before she could even complete the thought, her knees fell open so that Jasper could settle between them.

Her body hungered for *this*. For him. She hungered to take him *inside* of her.

In her mouth, to her breasts, into her very core.

And God help her, but she wanted to be conquered. She wanted to belong to a man––belong to *him*.

"Tilde." Her name sounded like a prayer on his lips. She opened her eyes when his mouth left hers.

Lifting onto his elbows, he studied her questioningly. He caressed her with his thumb: the side of her face, the corner of her eye, the ridge of her cheek. "I've ached for you." He shook his head, as though perplexed by—this.

His thumb grazed along her lower lip. "You don't know how many times I've wanted to do just this." He replaced his thumb with his mouth, a tender touch, a caress. Then he was driving deeper so that he could taste behind her teeth, searching, exploring.

Dear God but he'd conquered her—not with power or strength—but with tender need.

Adoration.

"I've been wanting to taste you everywhere."

She arched her back. When she let out a small cry, he captured it with his mouth.

* * *

His need for her had become an exquisite pain. And now to allow it free reign, God help him, but a ridiculous urge to weep swept through him.

He'd had urges, physical needs, but not sought out a means to satisfy them. He'd told himself it had been too soon. Perhaps he'd been fooling himself.

He'd wanted something magic. Tilde's name and face may not have been in the forefront of his memory, but he'd never forgotten the feelings he'd experienced that long-ago evening at Vauxhall.

He'd known there could be more.

And that *something more* was currently writhing beneath him, igniting the passion he'd been holding back.

He buried his head in her neck, inhaling the fresh scent of woman. Of this woman. He should resist her. Resist his desire. As these thoughts darted through his mind, his hand explored the tantalizing skin of her inner thigh.

She was an unmarried gentlewoman, gone into service. And her skin tasted like heaven.

She was his employee—whose silken hair fell between his fingers.

But most importantly of all, she was *Tilde*. She'd always been his magic. She'd always been *his*. And in that moment, rational thought ceased to exist. He needed her like a man in the desert required water.

He could not wait any longer. He could not stop. He'd not joined with a woman in nearly four years. Every ounce of blood he possessed had surged in a southerly direction.

As his fingers dared to part her feminine folds, he found her to be warm and slick.

"Tilde." He caught his breath. "You are untouched." Because she'd never married. She was a virtuous woman. And yet he watched her eyes while his hand touched her intimately. Even in the moonlight, he could see her pupils grow, making the greens and browns appear almost black.

"Tell me to stop," he groaned.

Her lips parted in a gasp as he pushed away his dressing gown and settled against her.

"I want this." She closed her eyes at the admission. "For so long."

He could no more deny the plea in her voice than he could deny that he'd wanted this since the moment she fell into that ridiculous tent.

But still, he knew this would not be easy for her.

"Tilde." Her name was a question. She nodded. "Stop me if…"

"Jasper." She almost sounded exasperated with him at this point. "Please."

Warm arms and legs embracing him. Silken heat beckoning his cock. He slid forward. When he met resistance, he inhaled and then broke through on a hiss.

Her arms tightened around his neck.

"I'm sorry." God, he remembered how Estelle had screamed and wept. He froze, hovering above this woman, awaiting her rebukes and curses.

None came.

"Tilde." He needed to see her face. Did she hate him? What had he done?

He drew back.

"Don't stop, Jasper." Her legs tightened around him. "Oh, please. Don't stop."

CHAPTER 13

CONSEQUENCES

*H*e'd stayed with Tilde until just before sunup. He'd been tempted to make love to her again but then punished himself for his selfishness.

The memory of her blood mingled with his seed stirred mixed emotions inside of him. She was not a young girl, a debutante, and yet she'd been an innocent. She'd given herself to him freely, holding nothing back. And, just as when he'd kissed her, he'd experienced both excitement and familiarity. He'd felt that joining with her had been something of a homecoming.

As he recalled the soft sounds of her cries, panting into his mouth, he found himself wanting her again already.

She'd reached for him in her sleep as he crawled from the bed. Unwinding her arms from around his neck, he'd taken a moment to share one last lingering kiss and crept from the room.

Years before he had married a duke's daughter and found a relative amount of contentment. But he later experienced pain he could not have imagined. He'd experienced guilt for not loving Estelle the way he'd wanted to.

He was determined to do things differently the second time around.

And so, on this fine morning, while he sat patiently allowing his valet to shave him, he began to form a plan.

He would fulfill his obligations in Parliament, make the requisite social appearances necessary to keep his mother happy. And he would marry Tilde. If she would have him.

Of course, she would have him.

Wouldn't she?

He'd do damned near everything he could to ensure she would.

He loved her and was relatively certain she felt the same.

His heart jumped at the thought. God, he hoped she would.

Having completed his morning ablutions, Jasper was ready to take on the world.

As per his routine, he would visit the nursery before going to the Palace. He'd see the children, his beloved daughters.

And as per his routine, he would also see her.

Only today he would not be forced to pretend she was only the governess to his daughters. Today he could allow himself to drink her in. He would reassure her, steal a kiss if given the opportunity. Whistling a jaunty tune, he made his way purposefully along the corridor toward the staircase.

She'd likely be blushing from head to toe when he saw her…

"You seem unusually pleased with yourself this morning."

At the stair landing, his mother stood unmoving, as though she'd been watching for him.

"Good morning, Mother." He nodded and made to pass around her.

But she stepped in the same direction, effectively blocking his way.

"I've been waiting for you, Willoughby. Can you spare me a moment before leaving for the Palace this morning?"

With a glance up the stairs, in the direction of the nursery, Jasper sighed. "What is it?"

She too, glanced along the corridor. "I'd rather speak with you in private. May we go to your study?"

"Can it not wait until tonight?" He was already close to being late.

"It really cannot." He noticed that she'd set her jaw, an indication that she would not give in easily.

Feeling resigned, he sighed. He would make every attempt to extricate himself from proceedings early on today. Perhaps the four of them could share another picnic if he came home soon enough. With Peaches. Mustn't forget Peaches.

"Very well." He conceded.

Frustrated at the delay, Jasper lead her into his study and impatiently took the seat behind his desk. She seemed in no hurry as she examined the rings on her hand for a moment before lowering herself into the wingback chair facing him. But then she only stared out the window, appearing unusually uncertain all of a sudden.

"What did you wish to speak with me about?"

"Your future, Jasper, and by definition, the future of the earldom." A determined glint entered her eyes. "It's time we make arrangement to send Miss Fortune and the girls back to Warwick Place. She has them well in hand, and you really ought to focus on making a match with Lady Elaine."

"For Christ's sake, Mother, Lady Elaine is naught more than a child. And besides–"

"If you prefer another lady, there is always Pembroke's gel. A bit long in the tooth but the Earl has posted an enormous dowry for her and that title is as distinguished as any. And of course, Lady Kathleen, Lemming's widow, is available."

"Mother, I'm not interested in any of them. And I most definitely have no wish to send my daughters away from me right now. With or without Tilde—Miss Fortune." He corrected himself.

His mother sat for a moment with pinched lips. "She is not the one for you."

Jasper drew himself up stiffly. Surely, she could not know…

"I believe that you think she is the one, with her pretty smiles and fine eyes. But you would quickly grow tired of her. Let us send her and the twins to Warwick Place tomorrow so that you can focus on a more equitable match here in town."

He would not dissemble. In this regard, he'd already decided to make his intentions known anyhow. He would have preferred to speak with Tilde first, but his mother needed to be set to rights.

"Miss Matilda Fortune and my daughters are to remain here with me. I have every intention of making Miss Fortune my wife."

At this declaration his mother burst from her chair. "That's preposterous, Willoughby! She's below us in every way. A governess? You obviously are not thinking straight. And if you were thinking with anything other than your nether regions, you'd have taken the time to investigate into her family. Her mother was a dancer at one time, Willoughby! A dancer! I wouldn't allow you to associate with them eleven years ago and I absolutely forbid you to have anything to do with her now. You are Willoughby and you shall marry accordingly."

His back ramrod straight, Jasper blinked at what he was hearing.

"You interfered before?" How had she even known?

"Did you think I'd allow you to throw this family's succession down the river by marrying a woman of such low birth? Because I know you. You've always been far too tender hearted for your own good. Even with Estelle, you would have allowed her to cease trying to provide you with an heir. Best for all of us that she's gone. She was weak. Despite all my urgings, she failed miserably at carrying out her duty."

The blood in his veins turned to ice. "Despite your urgings?"

A sick feeling followed the icy cold. Was his mother's interference to blame for Estelle's fixation on a son and her inability to love and accept their daughters?

"I merely emphasized that upon marrying you, she alone was responsible for providing you an heir. This was not anything new to her. Who was to know she'd weaken and die at such an early age?"

His mother's explanation was eclipsed by the warning Tilde had perceptively given him yesterday: *You do not see your mother. You must open your eyes, and your ears, and understand with your heart, who your mother is.*

How had he been so blind?

Jasper had never in his life hit a woman, but in this moment, he was close to striking his own mother.

He should have suspected her machinations all along. He'd wondered at times. But he'd persisted in the belief that his mother was a decent human being.

Step back and watch her... And what she is doing to your most precious treasures.

Damn his eyes. Was he to blame for Estelle's decline? And he'd been irritated by her obsession to beget him sons. He'd practically hated her for her refusal to embrace their daughters. And all along his mother had been dripping her poison...

He needed away from the woman he'd spent far too much of his life attempting to please.

"Stay away from my daughters and stay away from me. The dower house at Warwick is yours and I expect you to make use of it immediately. If that is unacceptable, I'm sure we can make one of the northern estates available to you." He scribbled a bank draft out. "This will cover your travel expenses and much more." He signed it with an angry slash.

Without another word, he pivoted on his heel and stormed out of the study. Roaring filled his ears as he reached the street and anger clouded his vision. Ignoring the manservant holding his mount, Jasper heedlessly marched along the pavement, not caring where he was going or when he would get there.

Damn Parliament.

Damn his mother.

And most of all, damn himself.

* * *

SHE AND JASPER had made love last night. He'd touched her everywhere and then joined his body with hers. It would likely be the only time she'd ever experience the act.

The thought nearly caused her to burst into tears.

Jasper.

He'd filled places inside that she'd never known to be empty. The feeling of being needed to such an extent by another person in this world, if only for a short while, was an overwhelmingly heady one.

"Will you read us a story before nap?" Tilde snapped herself back to the present. The children had been playing games with Peaches while Tilde stared at her notebook, not seeing a single word. Luckily, she had prepared her lesson plans for the morning far in advance, or she wasn't certain she could have imparted any substantial instruction whatsoever.

"It's Thea's favorite." Eloise explained, holding the book out with a cajoling expression dancing on her features.

"But of course." Smoothing her dress, Tilde rose and crossed the room. "Come now, Althea." Peaches jumped up and joined both girls, who had scrambled obediently onto Althea's bed. "All three of you."

Tilde made herself comfortable on the same chair she'd sat in last night... Before he'd carried her into her own chamber. He'd carried her!

"Miss Fortune." Eloise's voice jolted her again, for the umpteenth time that day. "You can turn the page now."

Tilde shook her head, as though she could shake every unnerving emotion out of it. If only so that she could manage to finish reading a simple children's story. "I'm sorry, sweetheart." She forced her mouth to read the words and did not look up again until she finished the last page.

Her actions last night had been unforgivable. They had jeopardized the security she'd begun to provide for these two innocent children.

What if he hated her now? What if he sent her away?

And then her heart raced at a most alarming thought. What if he'd gotten her with child?

At eight and twenty, Tilde did not labor under any misapprehensions as to the possible ramifications of what they'd done. She had approximately a fortnight to wait before she would begin to have an inkling if she was to be spared such a trial.

And then her gaze settled on the sleeping girls; Eloise curled behind her sister, Althea's arm hugging Peaches. Would it be so very horrible? Society certainly would label it as such.

Jasper was an *earl*.

An earl for Heaven's sake!

Earls did not offer for their children's governess, especially one who had chosen to act indiscriminately with them.

Ah, but it had not been indiscriminate. The true tragedy in all of this was that she'd done the unthinkable and fallen in love with him. If given the opportunity to express her love and to experience his affection again, she could not say no.

She would always have the memory of that night. She ought to regret it but what would that do? Assuage her guilt? Provide some personal form of punishment?

Foolishness.

She rose from her chair and tiptoed to the door leading to her own chamber. Recalling Lady Althea's nightmare of just last night, she left the door ajar so she would hear right away if either of the girls called out to her.

She'd made up her own bedding that morning after scrubbing at the soiled sheet with cold water. Now she pulled back the counterpane and breathed a sigh of relief that the stain hadn't set.

After making love to her Jasper had lain beside her until they both caught their breath. Then he had arisen and returned with a wet cloth. She hadn't expected that he would apply it between her legs himself. And, although embarrassed at the intimacy of his gesture, her heart had swelled even more.

He'd told her she would be sore today.

She drew the counterpane back up and focused on the unusual twinges she experienced now. The pain was ironic, the anticipation of relief bringing her only sorrow. She wanted to remember every moment for as long as possible. The pain served that purpose intimately.

She'd given a part of herself away that she could never get back––to a man who could offer her nothing in return. Not anything she could take, anyhow.

He was her employer. And now he'd been her lover.

After washing the stickiness from between her legs, he'd tossed the washcloth onto the floor and then held her. At the thought, she gasped and searched around the bed until her gaze landed on the discarded evidence of her impetuous actions. She scooped it up into her fist. What if the maid had entered and discovered it? Oh, but she could not rely on luck like this in the future.

He'd whispered tender words of appreciation and apology but not mentioned love.

She had not expected him to.

"Miss Fortune?"

Tilde spun around. She'd not heard any knocking at the door. Most definitely she had not expected to find Lady Willoughby standing just inside the threshold of her chamber.

CHAPTER 14

MY SON...

"*I* did not hear you knock." Tilde lifted her chin. Something in the woman's eyes made gooseflesh appear on her arms. In a horrified moment, Tilde quickly stuffed her hands, holding the soiled cloth, behind her back. "The girls are sleeping. Is there something I can do for you, my lady?"

Lady Willoughby's eyes narrowed. "I'm afraid that you and I must have a little... chat." The woman gestured for Tilde to take the only seat in the room.

Preferring to stand, Tilde declined.

"Very well, then." Lady Willoughby began. She sighed, as though already fatigued by whatever task she'd taken on for herself... "This is not the first time, and I fear it won't be the last."

"My son sometimes makes very poor decisions. And on occasion, they involve various members of our female staff, more specifically, our younger female staff. And inevitably, whenever he makes such a mistake, he comes to me. As his mother, I, of course, take care of these little *problems* for him. A mother does what she must. I'm sure you understand."

"Mistakes?" Tilde's mind required a moment to process what Lady Willoughby was saying.

The woman lowered her chin and raised her brows. "Ah, yes. Of which you hold the evidence in your hand behind you."

Tilde could do nothing to prevent the heat from travelling up her neck and into her cheeks. How did she know? She must have been standing in the door when Tilde scooped the cloth off the floor.

"Yes, mistakes, my dear. My son came to me first thing this morning. You are excused from your post—that goes without saying. If you choose to cause any difficulties, I'll be forced to report your unprofessional proclivities to the agency. Such a stain upon your references might make it extremely difficult to secure a respectable position in the future, would you not agree?"

Tilde struggled to comprehend exactly what the woman was saying. Not that Tilde was obtuse, by any means, but because the notion that Jasper had left her bed and then met with his mother…

But how else would Lady Willoughby have known?

The older woman held out a piece of paper. "He asked that I give this to you."

Tilde recognized his handwriting immediately. She'd found his barely legible scrawl almost amusing when she'd read over their contract.

The bearer of this draft is entitled to 3000L in exchange for her immediate withdrawal from Willoughby House. Signed, *Jasper Charles Talbot.*

"Willoughby expects you to take your leave before he returns this evening."

Tilde glanced toward the open door to the nursery. She thought she'd seen movement out of the corner of her eyes. Nothing was there.

"But what of the girls?" She could not help but ask the most obvious question.

Or was it? Lady Willoughby had shown time and time again that she cared little, or nothing for them at all.

Was this really happening? Jasper would not do this! He would not!

And then she remembered. His promises to call on her the morning after they first met. What had he told her was his reason for failing to come? That he'd been a fool?

Was this his reason now?

She stared down at his scrawled signature again, as though she'd imagined it the first time.

"Crabtree can stay with them until a replacement is found."

Tilde blinked and shook her head, as though she could somehow make sense of all of this by doing so. "But he…"

"Don't embarrass yourself, Miss Fortune, by begging and pleading your case. A woman your age ought to have known the ramifications of such unbecoming behavior. Besides, I've no wish to retain a governess with such loose morals for my granddaughters. There is no excuse for it."

Tilde stood stunned and then glanced around the room.

"I'll have a driver awaiting you downstairs within the hour. That ought to give you plenty of time to gather your belongings."

"I need to say goodbye to the girls." She could not leave Althea and Eloise without saying a word. She'd need to devise some sort of reason for abandoning them. She'd just promised them she wasn't going anywhere.

Lady Willoughby sniffed. "I suppose. But be quick about it."

And then she was gone, leaving Tilde holding a casually written slip of paper in her hand that changed everything she'd believed about Jasper Talbot.

Not magical.

Not wonderful. Not the most caring of men. Nor a father who put his daughters above all else.

She stuffed the paper into her apron and gulped down a sob. As badly as she'd have liked to rip the paper into several small pieces and throw them out the window, she had three younger sisters who depended a great deal on her. She'd decide what to do with it later.

He wanted her gone.

He'd done this before.

For now, what little time she had left, she would spend with the girls.

HAVING REFUSED THE DRIVER, *so graciously* provided by the Countess, Tilde stepped off the front step of the townhouse and moved aimlessly along the pavement. She carried only the valise she'd brought with her.

She had never allowed her heart to become so involved with any of her charges in the past. She vowed never to do so in the future. She ought to be leaving a trail of blood in her wake, she felt so very wounded and empty.

Making a fist of her right hand, Tilde ignored the sensation of loss. Normally Peaches would be tugging at her leading string, running in circles around Tilde's feet, or tying her up so that she could hardly move.

Tilde's eyes burned and she blinked away the stinging sensation. Saying goodbye had been harder than she could have imagined.

Eloise had cried but Thea had remained silent, clutching Peaches to her tightly.

Peaches has stared at her as though she was betraying them all.

And then worst of all, "Peaches, you won't leave me too, will you?" Thea had spoken into Peaches' neck. A shudder running through the girl's tiny body.

Tilde had done the right thing. Perhaps Peaches was the only reason he'd hired her. Tilde's small dog and Thea had bonded from the very beginning.

Tilde swallowed a sob that threatened to escape.

She'd known all along that their attraction to one another could amount to nothing and yet—fool that she was—she'd hope for more. She'd wanted to believe in magic.

She'd believed the love behind his gaze when he'd held her, when he'd kissed her.

When he'd buried himself inside of her.

Yesterday afternoon, Tilde had been happy. She'd seen real progress with both the girls. She'd had what she considered a mutually respectful relationship with her employer, a man she'd considered something of a friend. She'd had fulfilling employment.

She'd woken each day with the knowledge that she would see him. That she could watch him with his daughters and know that all of this mattered.

Yet today.

After one gloriously passionate night—everything had been torn away.

She would not grieve over the loss of her dog. Peaches would be loved and spoiled. Lady Althea and Eloise would have a loyal companion by their side.

He would not take that away from them.

Another sob rose in her chest.

Magic was not to be trusted. It was a cheap illusion. Madam Zeta's words echoed in her head. *Your First Kiss holds the answer to all that you desire.*

This time, instead of laughing out loud, silent tears rolled down her cheeks.

* * *

ONCE AWAY FROM the townhouse Jasper's thoughts cleared somewhat. He'd known of his mother's manipulations for years—he'd just not realized the extent of them.

He had been unwilling to consider how far she was willing to go. In his naivete he had believed his mother had visited Estelle to offer feminine support and comfort in the absence of his wife's own mother.

Quite the opposite. She'd been building Estelle's doubts even higher. *Damn his eyes*! He'd never questioned any of it. He ought to have seen his mother for what she was. He now recalled that when the terminal nature of Estelle's health had become apparent, she had departed Warwick Place and returned to London. She had abandoned them, rather than remain to offer comfort to a dying woman, to her granddaughters, to her son. And now he remembered receiving letters from her, hinting of women who, he now realized, she'd wanted him to consider as replacements for Estelle.

While his wife lay in bed waiting to die.

He'd been a clueless ass.

A sick disappointment replaced his anger as he strode unseeing through the streets of Mayfair. Had his mother always been this way? His father had been a mild–mannered gentleman. Upon examining his memories from a different perspective, he wondered if she hadn't taken advantage of his nature.

This morning Jasper had banished his own mother from London.

Was that really what he wanted?

He'd made love to Tilde the night before. He *loved* her.

She was the one. He had no doubt. What Jasper really wished for was to return to his country estate with his family. There, unencumbered by societal expectations of the ton, he could take Tilde as his wife. The girls would have a mother. He smiled for the first time since storming away from his house. His girls would have a pet.

He…

He would finally have his magic.

Tilde.

He did not wish to have his mother living nearby, in the dower property there.

Upon glancing up and realizing he'd made his way to Bond Street, he decided he'd meet with his solicitor. Stuart and Lords, the firm who'd handled his grandfather's affairs, his father's and now his own, housed offices just a few blocks down. He would meet with one of the solicitors and charge the man with finding a suitable residence in Mayfair for his mother. That way she would be no threat to Tilde. He'd not done well by Estelle. Although he could never change the past, that would be his burden to carry for a lifetime.

But—he vowed to himself–– he would protect Tilde and his daughters with his own life if necessary. He'd not allow his mother to poison their opportunity for happiness. Because that was something he wanted. Happiness, contentment. A life filled with love and laughter for all of them. And yes, there would be pain. There was always pain, which made it all the more imperative they embraced joy when it was in their midst.

He'd experienced joy last night. A piercing, all-encompassing joy that only comes with love.

Warmth filled his heart. She'd given herself to him so freely, with so much trust.

He should have believed the magic all those years ago. She had been the one for him then, she was the one for him now. But then he would not have the little lights of his life, Althea and Eloise. And he had loved Estelle. For a time.

But the time had come for him to guide his own future.

Damn all of society. Even if Tilde hadn't any claim to gentility, he'd still make her his wife.

The solicitors' sign beckoned. Just as he approached it an unusual sight drew his attention. A vaguely familiar figure of a woman was tying a mule to a hitch outside of the solicitor's office. It could not be! She was hunched over, wearing colorful silks and scarves, oddly reminiscent of––

"Madam Zeta." She was, indeed, the same woman who'd predicted his future less than one month ago. What had she told him? That he'd lost a fortune in his past… something about that fortune being his future.

He shook his head in denial. Was Matilda Fortune that fortune? The woman looked up just then and pinned her gaze on him. Yes, it was most definitely the same woman, with her dark skin and unnervingly light bluish grey eyes.

"Madam Zeta." He reached out to secure the tether for her and then flicked a coin in the direction of one of the young boys hanging about waiting for just such an opportunity. The woman seemed utterly out of place, with her mule, her colorful clothing and her dark skin.

But a determined glint burned behind those eyes.

"My Lord," she nodded respectfully. Did she remember him? But upon studying him intently, she twisted her mouth into a grimace. "You are close to reclaiming your fortune." She announced.

Was it possible? His smile froze on his lips. Even if it was not, he would humor the worn-out looking woman. Something he didn't quite understand compelled him to ask, "May I be of service to you?"

She flicked her gaze toward the solicitor's sign. "You are kind for asking. But no. Thank you." She reached out to him. "Give. Hand. Now." The same as she had before.

He didn't hesitate this time, curious as to what the woman had to say today.

She closed her eyes and took a deep breath. He waited patiently, ignoring the few odd stares they attracted.

When she opened her eyes, she blinked, as though coming out of a trance. "You stand to lose a great deal if you do not protect those whose hearts belong to you." And then she squeezed his hand in what felt like a warning. "We all have our paths and they are never clear. Do not dwell on regret, or unforgiveness. Happiness is within your reach." And then she dropped his hand, turned her back upon him and entered the stately office building.

Her predictions or fortunes or whatever he decided to think of them as unsettled him. She made sense in a way that perhaps could apply to nearly anybody. And yet, just now, he'd realized he needed to protect the girls and Tilde from his mother.

He'd ordered his mother to take her leave.

And then he'd walked away, leaving his mother alone in the house with––

He lifted his hand and hailed a hackney before he dared complete the terrifying thought. Happiness was within his reach. He would not take any chances this time. No, he was going to damned well take hold of it with both hands.

WHEN JASPER BURST into the nursery and saw Peaches curled up on Althea's lap, his first thought was relief. But when his gaze took in his daughters' tear–stained faces, a cold dread squeezed his heart.

Eloise rushed forward with a cry and threw her arms around his legs. "She left. Miss Fortune left!" Lifting his daughter into his arms, he steadied himself so as not to alarm her further. She was panicked –– trembling. This had to be the work of his mother.

"Hush, sweetheart. I'll bring her back." He carried her across the room and dropped onto the chair across from where Althea sat. "Surely, if she did not intend to return, she would not have left Peaches, now would she have?"

But Eloise was shaking her head. "She asked us to take care of Peaches for her. She said her new family probably wouldn't let Peaches live in their home. She said she was sorry and told us to be good for our next governess. But I don't want a new governess, Papa!" And then she buried her face beneath Jasper's chin.

Surely, Tilde had not wanted to leave! Was it possible he'd

been so full of his own satisfaction that he'd not realized she regretted the night they'd shared together? He'd promised her at the onset of her employment that he would not act on his inclinations and then he… had.

"Did she say why she had to leave?" Of course, she would not have told his daughters the real reason if that had been the case.

Eloise shook her head against his chest, but Althea looked up at him, and nodded.

"What did she say, Thea?" His silent daughter stilled the hand that was petting the small dog and squeezed her eyes together. He waited.

"The monster lady made her."

The woman in their nightmares? And then the terrifying epiphany her simple words evoked nearly brought tears to his eyes. Crabtree had been banished from the nursery.

The monster lady was his mother.

But his silent bashful little Thea wasn't finished. "You don't want Miss Fortune to go away, do you Papa?"

"Your grandmother told Miss Fortune that I wanted her to go away?"

Thea nodded. "But you don't, do you Papa?"

"You like Miss Fortune." This from Eloise, who'd lifted her head from his shoulder.

"I don't want her to go away." He admitted, his voice sounding thick. He loved Miss Fortune.

"Then you will find her and bring her back?" A fierce little light began burning in the back of Eloise's eyes. "Because she gave Peaches to me and Thea, but I know she's sad now."

"I don't want Miss Fortune to be sad." Large tears glistened in Althea's eyes, so very like his own.

Jasper lifted Eloise so that she was standing on the floor. "We most definitely do not want Miss Fortune to be sad. Your grandmother was horribly mistaken in what she said to Miss Fortune. Now, where are your bonnets and coats?"

As they realized he was taking them on the greatest of adventures, they both hopped up and rushed across the room to the large wardrobe. Jasper tied Peaches' leading string onto the pup's collar.

This time he wasn't taking any chances. His mother had ignored his orders, of this he had no doubt now. Jasper's children could not live peacefully within his own home until his mother was well out of the way. He'd need to visit Stuart and Lords again to make arrangements.

But first, he needed to find his fortune, and he knew precisely where she was.

Number thirty-six Wigmore Street.

CHAPTER 15

"*Y*ou left Peaches with them!" Betsy was all astonishment. Tilde would have been as well, had she considered doing any such thing just two weeks before.

When she'd arrived at her aunt's house, tearful and distraught, Betsy and Aunt Nellie had whisked her into their favorite drawing room, ordered hot tea and dropped a soft shawl around her shoulders.

"Lady Althea is comforted by Peaches. Peaches is the only person she'll talk to." Tilde made an attempt to explain why on earth she would leave her beloved pet behind.

"Dog," Betsy reminded her. "Peaches is a dog."

Tilde shook her head and moaned. It didn't matter. Nothing mattered right now.

Oh, she knew that she was going to have to pull herself together, but for now, the pain of leaving him… of leaving all of them, was too great to overcome.

"Of course, the children loved you. I won't even bother asking. And the Earl would not have hired you had he objected to your methods. It must have been Lady Willoughby then. I've never met a colder woman in my entire life." Aunt Nellie thanked the maid who'd entered and was setting down a tray of tea and then went to work preparing a cup just the way Tilde liked it. Three sugars and a splash of milk.

Tilde merely nodded and then took the cup from her aunt.

Yes, Lady Willoughby was a cold, cold woman, but had she been lying about her son's wishes? She had given Tilde the note written in Jasper's own hand.

The thought caused her eyes to begin stinging again. She had fallen in love with the blighter! Was he really such a fool as to leave the care of his daughters in the hands of Lady Willoughby? And to think that he hadn't even had the courage to send her away himself.

At such enraging thoughts, the stinging began to dissipate. In its place, a white-hot anger surfaced. She'd given him her virginity, for Heaven's sake. What kind of man took a woman's innocence and then sent her packing with a note for three thousand pounds?

She had gazed into his eyes while he'd been *inside* of her. And he'd held her so tenderly afterward. He'd whispered the sweetest words, even called her *love.*

And then it struck her.

Tilde was no fool where people were concerned––not usually. Had the note been some sort of forgery? The man Tilde knew Jasper to be would never had sent her away like that.

The message had not been from Jasper.

It could not have been.

When Tilde awoke to his kiss this morning––just before he'd crept out her chamber––she had felt *love* in his kiss. She'd seen *love* in his eyes.

She pulled the wadded-up piece of foolscap from her apron and unraveled it carefully. He had, indeed signed it. But… something had been torn from the top. A name perhaps? Was it possible everything Lady Willoughby had said had been a lie?

Of course, Tilde could not understand how the woman had known what transpired between Jasper and herself in Tilde's bedchamber the night before. But perhaps there was another explanation.

Lady Willoughby had entered Tilde's own chamber without knocking on more than one occasion. She'd also led Tilde to believe Jasper had plans to send the children and herself to Warwick Place so that they would be out of his way.

Jasper had said he'd considered the idea initially but hadn't pursued the plan.

Lady Willoughby most definitely was not to be trusted.

"I've left the girls alone with her." Tilde raised her fist to her mouth. "As well as Peaches."

"Do you think Lady Willoughby would harm them?" Betsy's voice echoed her own fears.

Tilde's stomach lurched at the thought. That woman would have no hesitancy harming an innocent animal… Or even the girls. Tilde replaced her tea on the tray and burst to her feet. "I need to go back."

"You cannot go alone." Betsy rose and removed the apron she wore over her simple muslin gown. "I'll come with you."

"And Crawford will go as well." Aunt Nellie offered the services of her long-term butler, an elderly but nonetheless intimidating manservant. "I'll have the coach brought around."

But Tilde was already marching toward the door. "I can't wait. What have I done?" With Betsy right behind her and her aunt signaling to Mr. Crawford, Tilde tore the door open wide and––

Charged directly into Jasper's arms. He grasped her by the shoulders, to steady them both. His black eyes filled with a new level of intensity.

"Tilde," his voice rasped her name.

"Miss Fortune! Miss Fortune!" Not only was Eloise jumping up and down, shouting her name in glee, but Althea was as well.

"Bark! Bark! Bark!" And Peaches joined in the melee, happy

enough to see her mistress after an entire afternoon of her absence.

But Tilde could not turn her attention to anyone but the man who'd pulled her up against him and seemed to have no intention of letting her go.

"What is all this commotion going on out here on my porch?" Aunt Nellie had come to the door. "Come inside before the neighbors begin making up stories." She shooed the girls in hastily and lifted Peaches off the ground into her arms. With a stern look in Jasper's direction, she added, "If you two wish to speak alone, you are welcome to use the front parlor. But leave the door ajar, mind you." And then she grasped Tilde by the arm in order to remove her from Lord Willoughby's grasp.

Stunned and more than a little relieved, Tilde was barely aware that Betsy had led the girls upstairs. Her aunt followed at a much slower pace, leaving Jasper alone with her in the foyer.

Reaching into her pocket, she pulled out the crumpled note and held it out.

"I won't keep it."

She could almost hear her own heart beating as he reached out and took it from her.

And then his brows furrowed and he was shaking his head.

"I gave this to my *mother*." His gaze practically bore into hers. "I demanded that *she* withdraw immediately."

Tilde wrapped her arms around herself. "She knew." Her voice came out barely a whisper. "That you spent the night in my chamber. Why would you tell her something like that?"

Jasper glanced around the foyer. "Will you lead me to this parlor your aunt has so generously offered for our use? Perhaps this is not the best conversation to have while anyone might overhear?"

Tilde supposed not, and yet--

"Why would you tell her?" She needed an answer first.

Jasper removed his hat and then ran one hand through his

hair. He apparently realized that an explanation was required before she'd consent to be alone with him again. "I did not tell her. She must have observed me leaving your chamber early. Or perhaps she guessed, God, Tilde, I would never tell her––or anyone––something so personal, so private between the two of us."

His voice begged her to understand. For the first time in so many hours, the horror of the day's events began to slip away.

She gestured toward the parlor. "Right in here."

Before she could take a step, though, Jasper swept her into his arms. "I was going to wait, to ask you. I wanted to try to set matters right. My mother is the monster, Tilde. She is the monster lady in the girls' dreams. Eloise says that she never struck either of them, but I'm terrified to allow her in their lives. I was planning to send her away. And then I plan on marrying you and taking you and the girls back to Warwick Place. I wanted to plan all of this out but when I arrived home, you were gone."

His words spilled out of him as though he was afraid she'd evaporate at any moment.

"And then Thea talked! She told me my mother had sent you away, that my mother had told you it was what I wished. And I was afraid you would not forgive me. I've made so many mistakes through the years. I couldn't wait another second to set the record straight."

But Tilde had pulled away. When she looked into his eyes, she saw all the emotions she'd been feeling for him reflected back at her. Lifting one hand, she silenced him with a gentle touch to his lips. "You plan on marrying me?" she spoke the words in awe.

He nodded. And there, standing in the middle of her aunt's aging parlor declared, "I love you. For what it's worth. Will you Tilde? Will you marry me?"

She touched his lips again. "It is worth a great deal to me." And then she smiled. "And yes. I will marry you."

He closed his eyes and released a deep sigh of relief. "We've missed all these years."

"I wouldn't have it any other way."

Jasper opened his eyes and stared back at her in confusion. "It was magic, when I met you, you know. I was simply too foolish to know how lucky I was to find it––to find you."

"It was." She smiled up at him. "But I am so very grateful to the woman who was your wife. I love your daughters and I love the father you've become. Perhaps it was fate that we go our separate ways and learn the value of love and its magic before we discovered one another again."

"He laughed out loud and lowered his forehead so that it rested against hers. "Do you believe it was magic? Or Fortune? Or Fate?"

"All of the above, my love. All of the above."

THE END

OTHER ENCHANTING STORIES by Annabelle Anders can be found by visiting her website or following her on social media.

www.annabelleanders.com
Bookbub
Website
Goodreads
Facebook Author Page
Facebook Reader Group: A Regency House Party
Twitter

Turn the page and read a sample of the next Fortunes of Fate Book written by Christina McKnight.

A SAMPLE OF THE NEXT FORTUNES OF FATE BOOK

FORTUNE'S FINAL FOLLY

*P*rologue
Oxfordshire, England
December 1814

THE BLUSTERY WINTER winds whipped at Madame Zeta's thick woolen cloak, pulling at the tattered folds and allowing the bitter cold to reach beneath to the thin cloth of her worn blouse and skirt. The severe English temperatures during the harsher months had ceased to affect her from the day her daughter, Katherina, was ripped from her bosom.

Nothing—not her lack of a home, threadbare blouse, matted hair, nor her worn boots—caused her any pain. She lacked far more essential necessities than mere possessions. Her heart had been stolen from her.

Before, the organ had beat with such vitality she'd feared her chest could not contain her love. Now, it was empty. Barren. Devoid of anything but hatred, loathing, and a determination borne of years of endless searching, relentless longing, and sleepless nights spent dreaming of her revenge.

From her spot atop the crest of the property, she glared down at the entrance to Shrewbury Gardens.

It had once been a place she'd longed to live and raise a family with her husband, Pierce.

Yet when she'd arrived, that dream had been stripped from her as quickly as her name.

After so many years under the guise of *Madame Zeta*, she'd likely not recognize her old name if someone uttered it…not that anyone but Lavinia knew her true identity.

A'laya De Vere, the Countess of Holderness.

Although, since she'd received confirmation that the duke had died, leaving his only son, Pierce as heir apparent, she was now the Duchess of Shrewbury—if she ever wanted to claim such a tarnished title.

She scoffed at the thought.

She'd rather perish than take the name and title of a man she despised. Never would she be known as anything but Madame Zeta.

But what she would not give to be plain Miss A'laya Banesworth, daughter of an impoverished baron from Nottinghamshire, England. Cherished offspring of Eugene and Chloe Banesworth, Lord and Lady Oderton. If she'd listened to her mother's warnings and not fallen under Pierce's treacherous spell, she never would have wed the then-earl, left her family estate, had his child, found herself abandoned, and her babe stolen from her bosom.

Her chest tightened, as it often did when she allowed her thoughts to meander down the path of her final day living as a proper lady at Shrewbury Gardens.

If she hadn't been such a senseless fool in her youth, Zeta would still possess a heart. She was thankful that her mother hadn't lived long enough to see how shortsighted and simple Zeta had turned out to be.

Unfortunately, she didn't have the guile necessary to prevent her world from shattering right before her eyes. Her own mother —living or not—would have been just as helpless where the old Duchess of Shrewbury was concerned.

Zeta had paid the hard price for her folly since the day she had taken to believing Pierce's lies and trusted his mother to care for her and Katherina.

"My child." A hand, light as a feather but as familiar as anything landed on Madame Zeta's shoulder. "Have I failed ye?"

She turned toward Lavinia, the old woman who'd been a mother to her since the day she'd taken Zeta in all those years ago. Starved, broken, and nearly dead, Zeta had wanted nothing more than to die when the Shrewbury coachman dumped her near Lavinia's caravan. However, Lavinia had told Zeta that one day, she'd reunite with her Katherina. Both women had held onto that declaration of fate. For Zeta, it was a deeply buried and sometimes painful hope, while Lavinia declared the fortune was a prophecy destined to come true.

In that moment, with Zeta battered and wrecked both on the inside and out, she'd decided to live…if only to see her daughter's face once more before her days in this world were up.

With each passing year, it was Lavinia who neared her end, not Zeta. And never did they get any closer to finding Katherina.

Unfortunately, she didn't possess a heart, if she had it would splinter ever more to see the kind old woman's steady decline.

How many times had Zeta insisted they journey to Shrewbury Gardens to see if Katherina had been brought back to her father's family home? How many times had Lavinia joined Zeta on the very crest they now stood upon, overlooking the place Zeta had expected to call home? No, not Zeta. *A'laya* had longed to call Shrewbury Gardens home. But A'laya and her tendency to see the good in everyone was gone.

Forever.

Madame Zeta was wise enough to know that if she ever expected to see her daughter again, *she* needed to find her. And as things had often been for Zeta, nothing came easily or without great effort.

As they stood on the ridge together this last time, Lavinia's fingers tightened on Zeta's shoulder. "I never meant to fail ye, me dear girl."

"You haven't failed me," Zeta mumbled, setting her hand on Lavinia's cold fingers and squeezing gently. "I have failed myself —and Katherina."

"Soon, I will be gone. But your time, and your search, are far from over."

"No—"

Lavinia tsked at her denial. "It is the way of things, the path of life, as ye very well know."

At Lavinia's words, the necklace, the only thing left to Zeta from her old life besides her heartbreak, warmed at her throat.

They'd traveled, the pair of them, all over England and Scotland. In their journeys, they spoke—sometimes huddled in a freezing wagon bundled in hides, one time before a roaring fire in the early evening outside London proper, and more recently on the coast of Dover during a particularly warm spell amid summer—of the day she'd be reunited with Katherina. In none of their musings had Lavinia not been by Zeta's side when *they* located Katherina.

Together. The pair of them. As they had been since the woman had rescued Zeta from the roadside and taken her in with nary a question.

Lavinia's steady stare scanned the expansive green grounds of Shrewbury Gardens, knowing the hellish torment Zeta had endured at the hands of the estate's cruel mistress, though Lavinia was always too compassionate to speak of it aloud. "I still feel, to me very soul, that your Katherina will be returned to ye."

"As do I." Zeta had spent all her adult life gifting fortunes to those who could spare the coin, and to many who couldn't. She'd learned much from Lavinia, including a knack for reading people

—their desires, their fears, and their hearts. "I will never stop searching."

"That is good, my child." The slight weight of the woman's hand slipped from Zeta's shoulder, and she felt Lavinia slipping from this world. Each day passed with Zeta knowing it was one less day with Lavinia near.

The shrubbery to their left rustled, and a woman not much older than Zeta appeared.

"Return to camp," Zeta whispered to Lavinia, nodding back down the hill to the wooded area that gave their caravan refuge from onlookers. "Seek warmth. I will return shortly."

Lavinia stared at the woman as she approached but thankfully acquiesced, turning slowly to return to the others.

"My lady?" The new arrival hurried over to Zeta. She dressed in the Shrewbury servants' garb, with her limp, brown hair tied at the nape of her neck. Beads of sweat formed on her forehead despite the late December cold. "My lady, is that you?"

It had been years since Zeta was mistaken for a lady, despite being raised to take her place in the upper crust of London society.

"Lady Holderness?" the servant said, stopping before her, her eyes narrowing on Zeta. She took in Zeta's disheveled appearance, though she must have found something she recognized as her stare settled on Zeta's weather-worn face.

"I have not gone by that name in many years. But, yes, it is me." Zeta glanced around, fearful that her husband, the wretched rakehell, would have someone near to detain her—or expel her from Shrewbury land. "Who are you?"

"My lady, I was the one who—"

Memories returned much like a dagger to her soul. "You helped the duchess collect my things before I was thrown from... Shrewbury." She nearly said her "home," but the estate below had no more been her home than the wagon she'd been traveling in for nearly two decades.

Her home had been with her mother—and later, with Katherina.

The woman dipped her head, clearly ashamed. "No, my lady. I, in no way, wanted to help the duchess. But I had no choice. Was never given a choice if I wished to keep my position."

Zeta eyed the woman, knowing she spoke the truth, yet unwilling to allow her actions to be forgiven so easily. "Where is my daughter?"

The servant's stare returned to Zeta's. "I do not know. I am merely a maid at Shrewbury."

"My husband then?"

The woman's cheeks flooded white, despite the chilly winds. "Last time word came to us, he was living on the Continent after a sordid incident in London."

"He has not returned since his father's passing?"

"No, my lady, though rumor implies he might have gone the way of the duke and duchess." Her tone lowered to a whisper before she continued, "may the Lord bless them in their eternal slumber."

Zeta nearly snorted at the maid's mumbled prayer.

"Who cares for the estate in Lord Holderness's absence?" she prodded, not allowing herself to dwell on that morsel of information. "There must be someone, a cousin or distant relative, who has come forward to claim the title and lands."

"No, my lady. Lord Holderness, err the Shrewbury heir, has yet to claim his title. However, no one disputes that he lives. No one who matters, that is," the maid replied. "Our salaries are paid by the steward. Some of the servants have been released from their posts. Only a few, those needed to maintain the Gardens, have remained. I have heard the steward is in contact with a solicitor in London."

"I should like to speak with him, the steward." Zeta nodded to the woman. She was, after all, Pierce's lawful wife. In his absence, perhaps she could… "Take me to him."

The maid shook her head. "I fear you are not welcome at Shrewbury. The duchess made that very clear before she passed, and the servants were reminded of her decree when you visited the duke several years ago. The magistrate is to be summoned if you even so much as set foot on Shrewbury land."

Zeta's shoulders stiffened as cold outrage settled in her gut. She shifted to stare past the maid to the estate below. "Has the magistrate been called then?"

How had she ever believed she could raise her daughter in such a bitter, unwelcome place, where even the servants feared for their future?

Though she desperately wanted to locate her daughter, Zeta could not jeopardize Lavinia and her people. They'd taken her in, fed her, and given her a place to sleep. She would not be responsible for their presence being reported to the magistrate—and whatever would likely, and swiftly, follow for Zeta daring to defy the duchess's final wishes.

"Of course not, my lady." The servant wrung her hands, her widened stare pleading with Zeta to believe her. "My name is Augusta. I have seen you watching but was unable to come and speak with you."

"Why do you wish to speak with me now? What has changed?" Zeta was not foolish enough to take the servant at her word, not after her employer's betrayal. "I have returned to Shrewbury as often as possible, yet no one has ever offered me help."

"The servants…" The maid bit her lip and clenched and unclenched her hands at her sides. "The servants are afraid."

"Of what?" Zeta demanded.

"Not what, my lady. Whom." She glanced over her shoulder and down toward the manor as if fearing she'd been overheard.

With the duchess gone, there only remained one person to fear. *Pierce*. "And you are not frightened of his wrath?"

"I was for many years, but I have never forgotten your daughter..."

"As I have not," Zeta snapped.

"I wish to help you find her."

Zeta was still unconvinced that the maid had anything to offer.

"Why *now*? When you never helped before."

"I couldn't interfere before with the duchess present. Now, with the duke and duchess gone, it is different. The servants, all of us, are worried about our positions. If the duke's son does not return to his place, what will happen to the lot of us, and Shrewbury? The steward cannot keep paying the servants as he does, with no lord presiding over the house."

Tension stiffened Zeta's shoulders as she reminded herself that the people of Shrewbury were not her concern. Perhaps, in a time long gone, they were. But not now...not ever. Only the thought of finding Katherina drew Zeta to Shrewbury, not any misguided affection or concern for the estate's servants.

"I can listen around Shrewbury. Mayhap ask after the babe."

Zeta narrowed her eyes on the maid, daring her to toy with her emotions a second longer.

"I am not the only one who remembers you and the child. Others were never loyal to the duke and duchess, though none will openly admit it. I can convince them. Together, we might be able to find her."

Zeta had never been blessed with anything even close to good fortune—if that were even what Augusta was bestowing upon her now, and not another falsehood or thin thread of hope that would soon be severed. Her mind told her to disregard the woman and renew her search, yet her heart...her heart pushed her to accept this simple kindness, even if the maid's offer proved fruitless in the end.

"I can send word to you if I hear anything," the woman promised. "It may take time, but I have faith that someone will speak on the matter. Someone will know what has become of your daughter."

"Thank you. I will return to Oxfordshire as often as possible," Zeta offered. The only bit of information she'd been able to gain since the duchess had thrown her from Shrewbury was the mention of a Vicar Elliott. The name had proven useless time and time again. In all her travels, Zeta had never found anyone by that name, nor met a single soul who knew of the vicar or his family.

However, hope—no matter how small—would not escape Zeta's grasp.

Long ago, she'd pledged to find Katherina, or die trying.

She was not ready to die, nor had she given up on locating her daughter—not in all the years she'd been searching.

CHAPTER **One**
London, England
September 1821

LORD JOSHUA STUART, second son of the Duke of Beaufort, leapt down from his carriage outside his Cheapside office and signaled for his driver to depart. Discarded morning papers and scraps of waste littered the hard-packed street, and two filthy, ragged mutts scavenged for their next meal. The shingle overhead squeaked, and Joshua made a mental note to oil the hinge and polish the tin signage that read simply: *Solicitor*.

The morning was warm, signifying that the afternoon would likely prove sweltering in the tiny confines of his office. It was days such as these that Joshua longed to help all those in need at his proper office off Bond Street. However, those less fortunate, the ones who needed to work every waking hour to keep the pantry stocked, the butcher paid, and the tallow burning, hadn't the time nor the funds to journey across town to the solicitor's office Joshua's uncle had opened nearly thirty-five years ago.

Joshua took his key from his pocket and slipped it into the hole, noting not for the first time the resistance when he turned it. With a bit more force, the key turned, and Joshua entered his building. The bell he'd hung overhead rang as the door swung closed behind him.

His assistant, Henry Portstall, was not due in to work for another hour or so. It was Joshua's routine to arrive early, sort through his tasks for the day, and spend a few minutes alone before the day grew hectic.

Unlike his Bond Street office, this small room, and the even smaller back office cluttered with client folders and reference volumes, was his sanctuary away from everything he found distasteful about the lives of his *beau monde* counterparts.

Here in Cheapside, Joshua was known merely as Mr. Joshua Stuart, Solicitor.

He was not the son of a duke, nor a lord above his neighbors and other small shop owners, in Cheapside.

Those who lived within walking distance came to him for contracts, negotiations, and many times, simply for advice. Tenants wronged by a landlord. A shop owner seeking the proper dowry befitting his daughter. Or a young, unwed mother needing information on education for her son. In all matters, Joshua was confident he could help those who sought out his help. And he did.

Joshua relished the days he was free to spend away from Bond Street. These were the people who really needed his help.

Pausing to light the several candles lining the front room, Joshua smiled as he made his way to the back office where he kept his desk. Shelving units lined the walls, holding his pocket watch collection and an assortment of large books dedicated to the study of English law.

His uncle, Lord Michael Stuart, had always droned on and on

about the one thing a man could never get back: time. Time to spend with his family. Time to pursue passions and activities he enjoyed. And, most importantly, time for the betterment of others and the world at large.

It was the sole reason Joshua had opened the small office here after his uncle's passing three years prior. He'd visited the area often for business matters, and when the small building had become available for purchase, he'd leapt at the opportunity. Never once had he regretted the decision or the financial investment he'd made.

Along with both offices, his uncle had entrusted him with his priceless watch collection. . Joshua stored most of them at his townhouse, but he kept a few less valuable, yet no less meaningful, pieces in Cheapside to remind him of the path he'd chosen in life.

An existence of servitude to those in need.

Starkly different than the life of luxury and leisure his elder brother, and their father before him, had chosen. Joshua silently chided himself. He gained nothing from dwelling on his family's excessive lifestyle, nor reminding them of those who lived lives so much less fortunate than they did.

The bell chimed above the front door.

"Good morn," Joshua called. "Please, have a seat. I will be with you momentarily."

He picked up the sheet of paper Henry left on his desk each evening and scanned the list of appointments scheduled for the day. Oddly, his first meeting wasn't until just before noon, though Joshua never turned away an unexpected client when time allowed.

Returning to the front, a courier waited patiently inside the door, clutching a familiar envelope.

It was the same as it had been since he'd taken the position with his uncle's office. Every three months, a courier arrived with an envelope to be delivered to Vicar and Mrs. Elliott at their residence in Cheapside. Their home was located above a small schoolroom, a few doors down from the vicar's parish church. It was how Joshua had stumbled across his current office in the first place.

That had been five years ago when he first met Vicar Elliott, his wife, and their daughter, Miss Katherina Elliott—or as the young woman preferred, just *Kate*.

"Missive for you, my lord." The courier handed the envelope to him and disappeared out the door once more, his satchel, heavy with his daily deliveries, slung over his shoulder.

Scrawled on the outside of the missive was:

Miss Katherina Elliott
C/O Lord Joshua Stuart, Solicitor

After Miss Kate's parents had passed away, her father only six months after her mother, the envelopes had come addressed to Kate, the surviving Elliott. He'd always known the parcel held pound notes, but from whom and for what purpose, he did not dare ask. It was not his concern, something his uncle had reminded him of often.

However, it *was* Joshua's responsibility to see the envelope delivered in a timely manner and unopened. And so, when he arranged his new office, Joshua had instructed the courier to deliver the quarterly parcels to Cheapside for a swifter delivery to Miss Kate.

His uncle had been a meticulous recordkeeper, and Joshua suspected if he truly wanted to know who the parcels came from and what their purpose was, he could find out. However, privacy and confidentiality were things born and bred into any man who took his position as a solicitor to heart. Which Joshua certainly had since his days at Oxford, learning the law from many great men who'd taken their oath to serve.

He glanced out the front window and across the street. A tall, light-haired man, finely dressed for Cheapside, loitered outside the cobbler's shop. His attention seemed focused on a stack of papers clutched in his hands as he read, nearly leaning against the building, but straight enough as to not sully his coat.

Two shops down from the man, the door to Miss Kate's schoolroom was open, and two young boys entered for their daily tutelage, a girl carrying a jug of milk not far behind. After her mother had passed away, Kate had taken over teaching the local children, those blessed with the opportunity to attend school instead of working alongside their families. In return, in lieu of tuition, her pupils gave their teacher fresh eggs, milk, bread, and fabric.

Slipping the envelope under his arm, Joshua left his office, locking up behind himself, and started across the street. The stranger did not turn in his direction nor notice the butcher's wife who'd exited her shop to sweep the walk.

Joshua straightened his jacket lapel and checked that his hair was not ruffled with his free hand.

To say that having Miss Kate Elliott close was an added benefit to renting the building in Cheapside was not worth dwelling on. The elusive draw that always had him staring out the front window in hopes of gaining even the tiniest of glimpses of her was beyond his ability—out of his control—and something Joshua could not deny himself.

He'd longed to invite her to join him for a meal or perhaps a carriage ride to Hyde Park. The friendship they maintained was not to that level. More's the pity. They'd been acquainted through his uncle's solicitor's firm for years, and neighbors after he'd rented his office across the street from her schoolroom, but neither had dared to go any further.

A wave. An afternoon chat. Once or twice a shared cup of tea while her students worked, but never more.

That did not stop Joshua from taking every opportunity to speak with Miss Kate. To ask after her day, to offer help with her students, or to simply be near her. Even if that meant visiting the cobbler next door to her schoolroom in the hopes of catching her eye as he walked past and having her invite him inside for a few moments while the children attended to their lessons or read books in silence.

Voices rose from within the schoolroom housed below Miss Kate's small residence that she'd once shared with her parents, though it wasn't the laughter or conversation of her pupils.

One most certainly belonged to Miss Kate, but the other was deep, loud, and...*angry?*

It was not the raised, happy voices of children Joshua was used to hearing floating on the breeze or in through his open office windows and door.

Joshua quickened his steps, peering into the darkened schoolroom as his eyes adjusted to the dim interior.

The children who'd entered as he departed his office wiggled past him and headed back outside. The milk from the jug the girl carried sloshed over the top and nearly splashed the leg of Joshua's trousers, but it saturated the front stoop instead.

"Sorry, Mr. Stuart," Sally Ann said, dipping her head.

"No worries, little miss." He chuckled. "They can be washed as easily as the floor. Who is with Miss Kate?"

"Ol' man Cuttlebottom. And he be right miffed, he is."

Joshua glanced around the schoolroom but Miss Kate and Cuttlebottom, the cobbler from next door, had moved out of sight into the back area. The spare space was used as a storeroom of sorts for supplies and other learning necessities.

"What is he upset about?" Joshua knew that children, though seemingly unobservant, listened intently when they suspected that something was afoot. Joshua had done much the same when he was young, especially when his father and grandmother embarked on one of their loud rows.

"He comes all the time to call and pester Miss Kate," Sally Ann whispered. "And he smells worse than the butcher shop."

True enough. There *was* a slightly pungent aroma in the room.

One of the boys tugged at Joshua's jacket. "He be want'n Miss Kate's schoolroom for hisself. I be have'n half a mind to thump the old bloke somethin' good."

Joshua stared at the children who'd gathered around him, silently waiting for him to handle the situation. He recognized some of the young ones by name, and others only by sight.

"The lot of you wait here." He gave the group a reassuring smile. "I am certain I can settle the matter for Miss Kate and Mr. Cuttlebottom."

Kate had never told Joshua that she was having an issue with anyone, let alone the cobbler. And wanting Kate's schoolroom and residence? Bloody hell, Cuttlebottom had been Vicar Elliott's close friend, and his grandchildren had grown up attending this very schoolroom.

Joshua made his way around the rows of tables with their benches pushed in, Cuttlebottom's voice growing noisier and harsher as he neared.

When he stepped into the back room, Miss Kate stood facing him, her hair swept high atop her head in a severe knot with a few stray curls escaping, her hands on her hips. Cuttlebottom shook his fist in her face, and Kate's bluish-grey eyes sizzled with warning as she took a step toward the old man.

"What is going on here?" Joshua demanded, moving between the pair. Cuttlebottom had no other option but to take a step back, his face molten red with fury. "Miss Kate"—he held up the parcel in hopes of defusing whatever had been transpiring between the pair— "I came to deliver this. The children said Mr. Cuttlebottom had come to visit you."

Her hands fell from her hips, and her expression morphed into her familiar, welcoming smile. Only Joshua feared it was a mask that she donned to diminish the severity of the situation he'd interrupted. "Thank you, Mr. Stuart. Mr. Cuttlebottom was readying to depart. He knows I teach class in the mornings."

"Shall I walk you out, Mr. Cuttlebottom?" Joshua offered when the man made no move to leave.

His glare remained focused on Kate as he said, "I know my way out, *Solicitor*." Cuttlebottom spit out the word as if he'd rather have called Joshua a colorful expletive. "But this is by no means over, *girl*."

The cobbler spun around, nearly tripping over his own feet as he rushed from the room in a huff, slamming the door to the schoolroom behind him.

"Thank you," Kate mumbled, busying herself with collecting a stack of primers from the shelf next to her. "Mr. Cuttlebottom can become quite nettled when the occasion strikes him."

"What was he enraged over?" Joshua paused before adding, "if you do not mind my asking."

Kate scurried past him, her arms full, and her gaze fixed on the uneven wood planked floor in front of her. "It is nothing. Truly."

His interest was further piqued by her avoidance of the subject. "It did not seem like nothing."

"He thinks my father should have sold the building to him before he passed away, that is all."

Joshua followed her into the main room as the door opened, and a dozen children flooded in. "And leave you homeless and without means to support yourself?"

"He claims my father promised him the building to expand his shop, but the paperwork wasn't finalized before my father's death."

Confusion must have been evident on Joshua's face because she asked, "What?"

"I handled all your father's legal dealings. He never spoke of selling the building to Cuttlebottom, or anyone, for that matter." Joshua thought back to his many dealings with the vicar. "He made arrangements for the building and all his holdings to transfer to you, along with a suitable allowance, until you wed." Joshua's body heated at the thought of Kate wedding.

She set the stack of books on the nearest table and called for Sally Ann to pass them out, before turning back to Joshua. "Until I wed." She laughed. "He was always a man of the old world, was he not?"

Joshua chuckled along with Kate, relishing the sound of her light laughter. His laugh was particularly light-hearted because Kate seemed put off by the preposterous thought of herself wedded to someone.

"He always said you were a man to trust, Mr. Stuart." She sobered, patting a young boy on the head as he took the seat closest to her. "He'd say, Joshua—savior, deliverer, salvation— how can a man of God not think highly of a solicitor christened with the name Joshua?"

"I can find no reason to fault your father's logic, Miss Kate," Joshua responded. "Speaking of delivery, as I mentioned, this parcel arrived for you today."

She eyed the envelope as he held it out to her. Her shoulders tensed, and she scrutinized the package before taking it from his grasp. She did the same each time he delivered one—as her mother had before her—and he reminded himself that it was not his place to question its contents or sender.

He cleared his throat, pushing his hand through his hair, likely mussing it. "I can speak with Mr. Cuttlebottom and seek a resolution on your behalf."

Kate's dark brows arched high. "A resolution?" she asked. "A resolution implies there is a problem or an issue that needs remedying."

"Seeing the man's anger moments ago would lead me to believe there is an issue at hand."

"Mr. Stuart…" She smiled, but it did not reach her eyes, and her tone turned severe, any hint of their earlier laughter fleeing. "It is a lark Mr. Cuttlebottom and I embark on every fortnight or so. He comes to my schoolroom, full of bluster, and shouts for a few minutes. Eventually, he calms down, says things are not over, and then leaves. He is old, and I dare say it is his way of expressing his feelings for the loss of his friend—my father."

Joshua glanced around the room as the children looked upon them with nervous energy. In no way did he feel that the situation between Miss Kate and the cobbler was simply a lark they played, no matter the tale Kate spun to distract him.

"He is a harmless aging man." She set her hand on his arm and squeezed gently. "Soon enough, he will forget it all and cease bothering me. Please, leave the matter alone."

Joshua inclined his head. "If you insist, Miss Kate."

"I do." Moving on from the topic at hand, she turned to address the class. "Children, what have you to say to Mr. Stuart?"

"Good morning, Mr. Stuart," they sang in unison.

The matter with Mr. Cuttlebottom was far from being settled, at least in Joshua's opinion. While he respected Kate's wishes, he did not trust the cobbler. No man had the right to badger or intimidate a woman, especially a fine lady as kind and selfless as Miss Katherina Elliott. Joshua would keep watch over the situation. If things changed—or progressed—he'd step in.

"A fine day to you all," Joshua responded. "I shall leave you to your studies. Please, listen to your teacher and apply yourselves to your learning."

"And mayhap," Kate called her students' attention back to her, "one day, some of you will study law and become a solicitor yourselves."

The children laughed and applauded, opening their primers to begin their lesson.

With one final glance at Kate, Joshua hesitated, uncertain whether or not he should leave the schoolroom with Cuttlebottom only next door. Kate was utterly alone in the world; her parents gone, and with no other family to speak of. He felt a measure of responsibility to see that no harm came to her. She spent every day in the service of others: teaching, counseling, and helping the children of Cheapside. She didn't need Cuttlebottom's threats shadowing her days. Nor did she deserve the cobbler's harassing visits.

It was a simple enough matter to handle. Joshua could pay Cuttlebottom a visit, have a few words and explain that as Vicar Elliott's solicitor—and now Miss Kate's—the cobbler could, and should, speak with him regarding matters such as the property belonging solely to Miss Kate. He would not discuss the specifics of Cuttlebottom's presence at the schoolroom nor demand he leave the woman be. Therefore, Joshua was not specifically going against Miss Kate's wishes, only notifying the cobbler that Miss Kate retained Joshua as her solicitor in all legal matters.

Joshua had made such calls before, both in person and via letter with his company signature. This was no different.

Kate slipped the envelope into the front of her apron, opened a book, and began reading to her pupils as each and every little face tuned into her every word.

If he stayed any longer, Joshua feared he'd fall in line with them, take a seat, and never leave, content to lose himself in the melodic lilt of Kate's voice as she read her tale.

He shook his head, gave the room at large a small wave, and departed, making his way down the walk to the cobbler's shop instead of crossing the street. He paused at the shop's threshold as the man he'd noticed loitering on the walk near the butcher's shop threw Joshua a quick glance over his shoulder and started off down the street in the direction of Vicar Elliott's parish.

Read the rest of Fortune's Final Folly!

Join the Fortunes of Fate Facebook Reader Group and play games! Have your Fortune told by Madam Zeta... Catch all the releases!

ACKNOWLEDGMENTS

Thank you to all the authors who participated in the Fortunes of Fate Shared World: Tabetha Waite, Nadine Millard, Diana Bold, Eileen Richards, Meara Platt, Amanda Mariel, Sandra Sookoo, Tammy Andresen, and especially, Christina McKnight!

And a HUGE Thank You to all the readers who joined the Fortunes of Fate Facebook Group and have cheered on each new release!

I love keeping in touch with readers and would be thrilled to hear from you! Join or follow me at any (or all!) of the social media links below!

Bookbub

Website

Goodreads

Facebook Author Page

Facebook Reader Group: A Regency House Party

Twitter

www.annabelleanders.com

Devilish Debutantes Series

Hell Hath No Fury

(Devilish Debutante's, Book 1)

To keep the money, he has to keep her as well…

Cecily Nottingham has made a huge mistake.

The marriage bed was still warm when the earl she thought she loved crawled out of it and announced that he loved someone else.

Loves. Someone else.

All he saw in Cecily was her dowry.

But he's in for the shock of his life, because in order to keep the money, he has to keep her.

With nothing to lose, Cecily sets out to seduce her husband's cousin, Stephen Nottingham, in an attempt to goad the earl into divorcing her. Little does she realize that Stephen would turn out to be everything her husband was not: Honorable, loyal, trustworthy…Handsome as sin.

Stephen only returned to England for one reason. Save his cousin's estate from financial ruin. Instead, he finds himself face to face with his cousins beautiful and scorned wife, he isn't sure what to do first, strangle his cousin, or kiss his wife. His honor is about to be questioned, right along with his self-control.

Amid snakes, duels and a good catfight, Cecily realizes the game she's playing has high stakes indeed. There are only a few ways for a marriage to end in Regency England and none of them come without a high price. Is she willing to pay it? Is Stephen? A 'Happily Ever After' hangs in the balance, because, yes, love can conquer all, but sometimes it needs a little bit of help.

Hell in a Hand Basket

(Devilish Debutante's, Book 2)

Sophia Babineaux has landed a husband! And a good one at that!

Lord Harold, the second son of a duke, is kind, gentle, undemanding.

Perhaps a little too undemanding?

Because after one chance encounter with skilled rake, Captain Devlin Brooks, it is glaringly obvious that something is missing between Lord Harold and herself… pas-sion… sizzle… well… everything. And marriage is forever!

Will her parents allow her to reconsider? Absolutely not.

War hero, Devlin Brookes, is ready to marry and thinks Sophia Babineaux might be the one. One itsy bitsy problem: she's engaged to his cousin, Harold.

But Devlin knows his cousin! and damned if Harold hasn't been coerced into this betrothal by the Duke of Prescott, his father.

Prescott usually gets what he wants.

Devlin, Sophia and Harold conspire to thwart the duke's wishes but fail to consider a few vital, unintended consequences.

Once set in motion, matters quickly spiral out of control!

Caught up in tragedy, regret, and deceit Sophia and Devlin's love becomes tainted. If they cannot cope with their choices they may never find their way back once embarking on their journey... To Hell in a Hand Basket...

Hell's Belle

(*Devilish Debutante's, Book 3*)

There comes a time in a lady's life when she needs to take matters into her own hands...

A Scheming Minx

Emily Goodnight, a curiously smart bluestocking – who cannot see a thing without her blasted spectacles – is raising the art of meddling to new heights. Why leave her future in the hands of fate when she's perfectly capable of managing it herself?

An Apathetic Rake

The Earl of Blakely, London's most unattainable bachelor, finds Miss Goodnight's schemes nearly as intriguing as the curves hidden beneath her frumpy gowns. Secure in his independence, he's focussed on one thing only: evading this father's manipulating ways. In doing so, ironically, he fails to evade the mischief of Emily's managing ploys.

Hell's Bell Indeed

What with all the cheating at parlor games, trysts in dark closets, and nighttime flights to Gretna Green, complications arise. Because fate has limits. And when it comes to love and the secrets of the past, there's only so much twisting one English Miss can get away with...

Hell of a Lady

(*Devilish Debutante's, Book 4*)

Regency Romance between an angelic vicar and a devilish debutante: A must read if you love sweet and sizzle with an abundance of heart.

The Last Devilish Debutante

Miss Rhododendron Mossant has given up on men, love, and worst of all, herself. Once a flirtatious beauty, the nightmares of her past have frozen her in fear. Ruined and ready to call it quits, all she can hope for is divine intervention.

The Angelic Vicar

Justin White, Vicar turned Earl, has the looks of an angel but the heart of a rake. He isn't prepared to marry and yet honor won't allow anything less. Which poses something of a problem… because, by God, when it comes to this vixen, a war is is waging between his body and his soul.

Scandal's Sweet Sizzle

She's hopeless and he's hopelessly devoted. Together they must conquer the ton, her disgrace, and his empty pockets. With a little deviousness, and a miracle or two, is it possible this devilish match was really made in heaven?

Hell Hath Frozen Over

(Devilish Debutantes, Novella)

The Duchess of Prescott, now a widow, fears she's experienced all life has to offer. Thomas Findlay, a wealthy industrialist, knows she has not. Can he convince her she has love and passion in her future? And if he does, cans she convince herself to embrace it?

To Hell And Back

(Devilish Debutantes, Novella)

The Duchess of Prescott, now a widow, fears she's experienced all life has to offer. Thomas Findlay, a wealthy industrialist, knows she has not. Can he convince her she has love and passion in her future? And if he does, cans she convince herself to embrace it?

Lord Love a Lady Series

Nobody's Lady

(*Lord Love a Lady Series, Book 1*)

Dukes don't need help, or do they?

Michael Redmond, the Duke of Cortland, needs to be in London—most expeditiously—but a band of highway robbers have thwarted his plans. Purse-pinched, coachless, and mired in mud, he stumbles on Lilly Beauchamp, the woman who betrayed him years ago.

Ladies can't be heroes, or can they?

Michael was her first love, her first lover, but he abandoned her when she needed him most. She'd trusted him, and then he failed to meet with her father as promised. A widowed stepmother now, Lilly loves her country and will do her part for the Good of England—even if that means aiding this hobbled and pathetic duke.

They lost their chance at love, or did they?

A betrothal, a scandal, and a kidnapping stand between them now. Can honor emerge from the ashes of their love?

A Lady's Prerogative

(*Lord Love a Lady Series, Book 2*)

It's not fair.

Titled rakes can practically get away with murder, but one tiny little misstep and a debutante is sent away to the country. Which is where Lady Natalie Spencer is stuck after jilting her betrothed.

Frustrated with her banishment, she's finished being a good girl and ready to be a little naughty. Luckily she has brothers, one of whom has brought home his delightfully gorgeous friend.

After recently inheriting an earldom, Garrett Castleton is determined to turn over a new leaf and shed the roguish lifestyle he adopted years ago. His friend's sister, no matter how enticing, is out-of-bounds. He has a run-down estate to manage and tenants to save from destitution.

Can love find a compromise between the two, or will their stubbornness get them into even more trouble?

A betrothal, a scandal, and a kidnapping stand between them now. Can honor emerge from the ashes of their love?

Lady Saves the Duke

(*Lord Love a Lady Series, Book 3*)

He thinks he's saving her, but will this Lady Save the Duke, instead?

Miss Abigail Wright, disillusioned spinster, hides her secret pain behind encouraging smiles and optimistic laughter. Self-pity, she believes, is for the truly wretched. So when her mother insists she attend a house party —uninvited—she determines to simply make the best of it…until an unfortunate wardrobe malfunction.

Alex Cross, the "Duke of Ice," has more than earned the nickname given him by the ton. He's given up on happiness but will not reject sensual pleasure. After all, a man has needs. The week ought to have been pleasantly uneventful for both of them, with nature walks, parlor games, and afternoon teas on the terrace…but for some inferior stitchery on poor Abigail's bodice.

And now the duke is faced with a choice. Should he make this mouse a respectable offer and then abandon her to his country estate? She's rather pathetic and harmless, really. Oughtn't to upset his life whatsoever.

His heart, however, is another matter…

Lady at Last

(*Lord Love a Lady Series, Book 4*)

She can't make a baby without a husband!

Or can she?

After witnessing the miracle of birth, self-determined spinster Miss Penelope Crone is having second thoughts about swearing off marriage. She wants – no, she needs – to experience the blessed event herself. Dear God, she's practically thirty! Time is running out!

Hugh Chesterton, Viscount Danbury, is relatively intelligent, good looking, unmarried, and most importantly, close at hand. With a little décolletage, a sway of the hips, and a few drinks of brandy, Penelope is certain she can extract a respectable offer.

If only she'd accounted for the power of passion.

Because unchecked lust takes over, leaving Penelope in a most precarious predicament. And Lord Danbury –– the goose-brained jackanapes –– is proving far less attainable than she'd imagined.

Is Penelope to be cast out of society or will Lord Danbury take a leap of faith and save her from ruin? He'd better act fast if he's going to make her his lady. HIs Lady At Last...

For more info on Annabelle's Books, go to

AnnabelleAnders.com

64264580R00104

Made in the USA
Middletown, DE
30 August 2019